APR   2010

Super

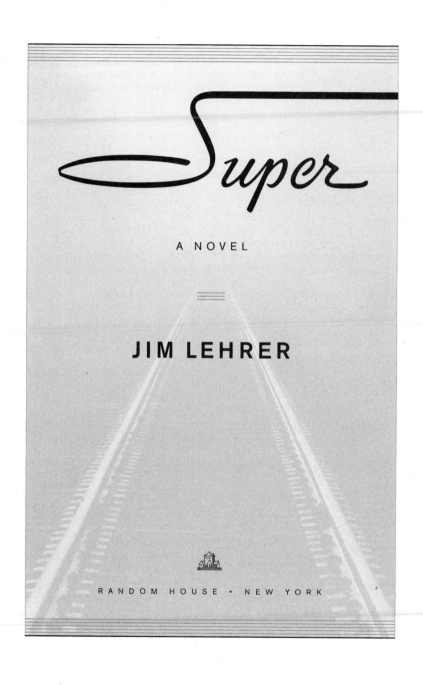

Super

A NOVEL

JIM LEHRER

RANDOM HOUSE · NEW YORK

Published in the United States by Random House, an imprint of The Random House Publishing Group, a division of Random House, Inc., New York.

RANDOM HOUSE and colophon are registered trademarks of Random House, Inc.

LIBRARY OF CONGRESS CATALOGING-IN-PUBLICATION DATA
Lehrer, James.
Super: a novel / Jim Lehrer.
p. cm.
ISBN: 978-1-4000-6763-3
eBook ISBN: 978-1-5883-6970-3
1. Super Chief (express train)—Fiction.   2. Passenger trains—
United States—Fiction.   3. Travelers—Fiction.   4. Murder—
investigation—Fiction.   I. Title.
PS3562.E4419S86 2010   813'.54—dc22   2009014448

Printed in the United States of America on acid-free paper

www.atrandom.com

2 4 6 8 9 7 5 3 1

First Edition

Book design by Victoria Wong

To the train people

Super

Dearborn Station, Chicago, was where the stories of the three Super Chief deaths began and ended.

They started with Dale L. Lawrence, a Private, slipping through a back door of the station crew's ready room and moving to Track 7 and then alongside the Super, as admirers called the Santa Fe Railway's famed streamliner.

Lawrence followed closely a porter named Ralph to a vestibule door, then up into a still-empty sleeping car.

Ralph had been reluctant to do business with this man, mostly because of his appearance. Not only was he sickly, his clothes were wrinkled and unclean. And he had no luggage. But the price was right, less than a full fare but better than nothing. Thirty-five dollars in cash was cheap for a ride from Chicago to Los Angeles on America's most luxurious all-sleeper train.

In the workaday language of the Super there were four categories of passengers—Privates, Strays, Regulars and Stars. A Private was a person who traveled as the result of a one-on-one deal with a sleeping car attendant. This longtime practice had begun during the travel conditions of World War Two. Cash money had a way of finding room on the most crowded of trains.

Now, in this April of 1956 with fewer passengers and plenty of space available, the attraction was a fare cheaper than the official one.

"This is yours," said Ralph, pushing open the door to a small roomette. "It will not be made up as a bed in case I need it suddenly for a Stray—you know, a passenger who pays a conductor for an upgrade or wants to change bedrooms."

Lawrence nodded to Ralph. He understood. But instead of speaking, he coughed. Ralph had heard the man, who appeared to be in his late forties, do little else but cough since they first met at Dearborn Station and made their business arrangement.

"Remember now, there could be conductors around at almost any time looking at tickets, so you must stay right here in this bedroom, sir," Ralph said. "I'll bring you a sandwich or something to eat after we leave the station and a roll with coffee in the morning. You do cream and sugar?"

The man shook his head but said nothing.

Ralph took a closer look at him. His brown suit, though to Ralph's trained eyes an expensive Nash Brothers', was slack and stained, his flowered tie away from the collar, his white shirt soiled, his heavy blond hair uncombed, his face, drawn and gray, with at least a day's beard.

Ralph said, "Well, if anyone but me should happen to knock on the door, hide in the bathroom and don't answer." He hit a knuckle on the door, then followed with two quick knocks. "That's my signal. One knock, pause, then one-two." He did the three knocks again. "You follow me?"

Lawrence nodded—and coughed again.

"You're going all the way to Los Angeles, right, mister?" Ralph asked as he prepared to leave the roomette, the smallest of the accommodations available on the Super. There were also bedrooms, drawing rooms and compartments of varying sizes, but mostly, every space was referred to as a compartment.

"At least until Kansas City," the man said.

Ralph shrugged, closed the door and went on with his other non-Private duties.

Here now was Clark Gable, a Star, coming down the station platform toward his sleeping car. A redcap named James was taking care of him and his luggage.

Darwin Rinehart, a Regular, felt a flash of joy and well-being—for the first time in months.

"Hey, King Clark!" he called out.

The King of Hollywood, as they called Clark Gable, jerked his head in Rinehart's direction but after only a glance turned back away. The message was unmistakable. But Rinehart chose to ignore it.

"Gable's not going to talk to you," said Gene Mathews, another Regular who was Rinehart's associate in the movie business as well as his best friend. "Don't humiliate yourself, for god's sake."

"Go ahead and get us settled," Rinehart said quietly to Russell, his own redcap. He and James would be handsomely rewarded for providing this special treatment of boarding the Super Chief early and privately—before all the other passengers. Rinehart had no idea, of course, that a Private had preceded even them a few minutes earlier.

Rinehart approached Gable while Mathews and James headed to the first car, half sleeping accommodations and a bar-lounge at the end of the Super Chief, which was backed into the platform for loading.

While the Super was still known and celebrated as the Train of the Stars, some of its Hollywood glitter had switched to airliners. Errol Flynn and his pair of lion-sized dogs that often traveled with him were long gone from the Super. So were William Holden, Cecil B. DeMille and Grace Dodsworth. Gloria Swanson, Claudette Colbert, Edward G. Robinson and Judy Garland were the major remaining Stars. Recently Judy Garland had even had a mock wedding ceremony performed by a Super engineer during a brief stop someplace in Arizona or New Mexico.

But the real Super fan, among the Stars, had always been Clark Gable. There wasn't a porter, steward, barber or conductor on this train who didn't have a Clark Gable story to tell, most of them concerning booze and/or women.

Gable was handing out cash to James when Rinehart got there. "Hey, King Clark, how are you, pal?" said Rinehart. He started to thrust out his right hand but decided against it once he saw that both of Gable's hands—known as the largest in Hollywood—and full attention were involved in the dispensing of money.

Barely flicking his head in the direction of Rinehart, Gable said, "Fine. I'm fine."

Rinehart said, "We came on the Broadway Limited from New York. Didn't see you. You must have come on the Twentieth Century—or another train. Right?"

Gable didn't throw even a glance.

"Maybe we could get a drink, maybe have a meal together tonight or tomorrow?" Rinehart persisted. "We've got forty hours ahead of us here on the Super before LA."

"I'm not going to get out much this trip. Got work to do." Gable stepped on the stool and up into the vestibule of his car, still without making direct eye contact.

Rinehart fell back a step, as if he had been physically pushed away.

Charlie Sanders, an assistant general passenger agent for Santa Fe, asked, "How many times have you ridden with us on the Super, Mr. Wheeler?"

Otto Wheeler, a Regular, sat in a wheelchair, no longer having the strength in his legs and lower body to take more than a few difficult steps on his own.

Sanders was there with the redcaps and attendants helping carry Wheeler up and into a drawing room in "Taos," as the rounded-end combination car was named.

How many times have you ridden with us on the Super, Mr. Wheeler?

Wheeler heard and understood the question. This nice young railroad man deserved an answer. Wheeler's first trips on this train of stainless steel silver beauty were when he was still a kid. His parents took him and his sisters to Kansas City and Chicago or, a few times, west to Albuquerque or Los Angeles. Then there were at least two or three times a year when he was at the University of Chicago and, later, at the Wharton School in Philadelphia. Since then, on business or pleasure, there were so many travels on the Super that Wheeler's friends had begun to refer to the train as his second home.

His trips had become almost obsessively frequent in the last four years.

Wheeler suffered from a terrible cancer that had begun as a sore throat. His face, once tanned and round like a happy pumpkin, was the color of white starch and resembled the face of an ancient ghost. His 205-pound body now weighed 135.

"One thousand four hundred and sixty-two," Wheeler replied. His voice was weak but still audible.

Sanders laughed. "I believe it, sir, I believe it—and then some. They tell me that if there was a world's record for riding the Super you'd hold it, that's for sure."

Wheeler was forty-two, single, religious and wealthy. His

money and religion came from his family, who owned most of the giant grain elevators that were the economic and geographical centers of the cities and towns in the wheat country of central Kansas. Wheeler lived in Bethel, a major Santa Fe Railroad division point between Wichita and Kansas City; its residents were mostly Randallites, a sect of early settlers escaping religious persecution in Europe.

Otto Wheeler was on his way home to Bethel now on the Super Chief.

"There's not one thing that gives the Super more pleasure, Mr. Clark Gable, than having you aboard its streamlined presence," said Ralph, sleeping car porter, as he placed Gable's suitcase on a shelf over the small closet in the drawing room.

Ralph had been shuttling back and forth among the compartments of Gable, Wheeler and the other passengers for whom he had the responsibility.

"Thank you," said Gable, after taking a short draw on the Kent he was smoking. He smiled but it was a nervous smile, something Ralph saw as unusual. The King was normally so at ease with him and most everyone else.

Ralph, still smiling as he moved toward the door, asked, "You'll be wanting dinner here in the compartment as always?"

Gable nodded. "As always, right."

"The usual, sir?"

"Yes . . . of course. The usual."

Ralph, keeping his real reactions to himself, said, "Good, good. That's good. The shrimp is particularly fresh and whopping for the cocktail, the double sirloin is red as ever for you to have it rare, the corn chowder is as good as ever . . ."

Ralph waited a beat for a response that didn't come. Then he said, "Red wine, of course. There's a fine new one from Bordeaux, I understand."

"Of course."

"Yes, sir. What time are you wanting to be served, Mr. Gable?"

When Gable didn't answer immediately, Ralph added, "Your usual time? Around nine?"

"Yes . . . of course," Gable said.

"Yes, sir. What about any beautiful Strays who may want to pay their respects on this trip?" Ralph asked matter-of-factly, same as with the food and drink, as if it was part of the routine—the ritual. A Stray was the term for any paying passenger who was not recognized by any crew member as a Star or a Regular.

"Maybe . . . Yes. Why not? Although, it's possible nobody'll even know I'm on the train."

Ralph chuckled. "Now, Mr. Gable, you know better than that. There's no way to keep The King a secret. It's almost like the word spreads from one end of the train to the other with the clicking of the wheels on the track. Clark Gable's on board,

Clark Gable's on board. The King is here, The King is here. Clickety-click, clickety-click, clickety-click, click, click."

Gone with the Wind and Carole Lombard's death in a plane crash had dramatically intensified the attention—and the opportunities. It went with being The King.

"I take it you want to wait awhile for me to make up the bed, sir, as usual?" said Ralph. It was his last question.

"That's right, as usual—everything the way you always do it," said Gable. "I'm just going to sit here for a while."

He reached down to a small leather briefcase and unbuckled it. He pulled out an opened carton of Kent cigarettes and then, one at a time, four bottles of Johnnie Walker Red Label scotch.

Ralph recognized them as being among Clark Gable's usual companions.

"This train, this lovely Super Chief, is the only place I feel safe anymore, Gene," said Darwin Rinehart. "How sick is that for a man my age?"

"Dead sick," replied Gene Mathews.

"This could be my last trip on the Super," Rinehart said. "How sad is that to think about for a man my age?"

"Stupid sad," said Mathews.

He and Rinehart were sitting in the side-by-side lounge chairs in their drawing room. Rinehart told Mathews what had just happened with Clark Gable.

"It's not personal with Gable or anybody else out there. It's business. You know that," Mathews said. "They're afraid if they pay attention to somebody who's down they'll get sick with down, too. Down by association."

Down by reputation, too. And by failure. And now by humiliation, with everyone in Hollywood from Gable and the stars on to stagehands. Darwin Rinehart's biggest movie, *Dark Days*, had flopped so spectacularly that everything he had went down with it.

Now Rinehart didn't wait for Ralph to come back with the Beefeater martini—straight up with three tiny olives—that was his automatic onboard drink. Instead, he took a sip out of the thin silver flask of gin that he had stuck into his suitcase. The cast of *The Tie That Binds* had given it to him when the picture was nominated for an Academy Award in 1940. Their names were engraved on one side along with his.

Mathews said, "We've talked and talked about this. I'm sick of talking about this. It's only over for you in your head—not in real life."

Darwin Rinehart, still barely forty years old, had done well as a producer when he was young, run a successful studio and made several pictures that won great reviews and honors. He had escaped the Hollywood blacklist and Red Scare problems of the last few years because he was mostly a nonpolitical Republican who didn't know any Communists. But even so, he hit a string of bad luck on his movies, and nothing much good of any kind had happened to him lately even before the gigantic failure of *Dark Days*.

"I can't make a picture because everybody knows I'm a loser, I'm broke, that's the problem," Rinehart said to Mathews.

"Broke you are. Loser you are not. We could have flown back and forth to LA five times for what it's costing for this train setup. Going to New York to see plays you really couldn't even afford to see much less buy their movie rights was nuts."

"I always go to New York to see plays whether I use them or not and I will always go on the train—on the Super Chief— whether I can afford it or not. The Super is where I belong to the end."

"You're nowhere near the end, except in your bad dreams," Mathews said, turning his attention back to his book, *Elmer Gantry*, by Sinclair Lewis.

As much to the compartment walls and windows as to Mathews, Rinehart said, "They're going to take everything I have left. They've already got liens on everything at the studio—including my Brancusi. You know that."

Darwin Rinehart rubbed his right hand over his hairless head, made so by his twice-daily shaving. It was something he began five years ago after his premature baldness had removed most every other small sign of his graying dark brown hair anyhow. The story, often told with Rinehart's encouragement in movie magazines and elsewhere, was that the inspiration for the shaved head was the white marble egg-shaped sculpture by Constantin Brancusi that had become Rinehart's most treasured possession.

Mathews, whose head was covered in thick black hair combed straight back with the help of much Vitalis hair tonic, didn't even look up from his book. He said, "Television. How many times do I have to say this? Make a deal with one of the television networks, take the deal to the bank for some financing. That's what Loretta Young did and look at her. She's winning Emmys and making bundles of money."

"Traitor! She's a traitor to pictures!"

Ralph arrived with Rinehart's martini. Mathews, a recovering alcoholic, had a Coca-Cola. They asked Ralph to make a reservation for dinner in the dining car for eight . . . eight thirty, whatever worked.

"We'll wait for a table for two—by ourselves," Rinehart said to Ralph. "No shared table—always. Got it?"

"Got it always, Mr. Rinehart, yes, sir—always," said Ralph.

After Ralph left, neither said anything for a good four or five minutes. Mathews returned to Sinclair Lewis; Rinehart looked out the drawing room window at the Texas Chief, preparing to leave from the next track.

"*Dark Days* was not my fault," Rinehart said finally. "The script was a mess by the time we started shooting, Sol turned out to be a directing nightmare, the actors were mostly on dope, that dust storm blew up from Nevada to Utah on us at the worst possible time."

"I know, I know—I was there, too, remember."

"Same kind of problem for that awful John Wayne flop . . ."

"John Wayne as Genghis Khan, how could it have been anything but a flop," Mathews said.

"I meant the Utah dust."

Mathews nodded knowingly. Part of Wayne's awful movie had been shot in the same desert location just before Rinehart's.

"*The Conquerer* was his picture, his bomb," Mathews said. "*Dark Days* was your picture, your bomb. Just like the last three before. That makes four bombs in a row, which adds up to where you are. I'm sick of talking about this."

"Duke Wayne will survive *The Conqueror*, but Gable's as through as I am. When I saw him just now it looked like even his big ears were smaller. Hands, too. Everything about him is shrinking."

"Except his bank account," said Mathews.

"Money's only his third love behind booze and broads. He lives to drink and screw and if it hadn't been for *Gone with the Wind* he wouldn't be able to do either on this train or anywhere else. I hear Warner Brothers is after him to make a Civil War picture with Yvonne De Carlo playing a mulatto slave. It's a *Gone with the Wind* takeoff. Without *Gone with the Wind*, Gable would be nothing."

"That's like saying the Yankees would be nothing without DiMaggio. The Yankees *have* DiMaggio, Gable's *got* his *Gone with the Wind*. Do television."

"Never!"

Both became silent again until Rinehart, almost in a whisper, said, "Don't ever leave me, Gene."

"I won't, Dar," said Mathews. He spoke in his normal voice. "I've said it to you a million times. I'm tired of saying it."

"When you leave me, that's when I'll know it's really over."

"For the last time—I won't, Dar," Mathews said.

"Everything's for the last time," Rinehart mumbled out toward Track 8, where the Texas Chief was also preparing for departure.

Ralph returned to Otto Wheeler's drawing room. Charlie Sanders was still there.

"I see you're traveling alone, is that right, Mr. Wheeler?" asked Ralph, as he and Sanders helped Wheeler from the wheelchair into the dark green parlor chair that faced the room's large outside window.

Otto Wheeler nodded.

"What's your Mr. Pollack up to?" asked Ralph, referring to the assistant who often traveled with Wheeler in the next compartment.

"He went ahead yesterday to take care of some business for me," Wheeler said. "He's going to meet me at the station in Bethel."

Wheeler turned to stare out the window even though there

was not much to see except the Texas Chief and railroad employees passing by on missions involving one of the two trains. The Texas Chief, also a streamliner of gleaming corrugated lightweight steel, had been scheduled to leave an hour before the Super, at 6:00 p.m., for Fort Worth, Houston, Galveston and other points south. But it was already almost 6:20.

"They better get a move on over there or it'll slow us down—make us late even," said Ralph to Sanders before Wheeler had a chance to raise the point. "The Texas Chief goes right along an hour ahead of us on the same track past Kansas City into Kansas."

I know that! Sanders wanted to bark. But he remained silent. It seemed to Sanders that some porters, conductors and the other men who actually worked on the trains couldn't resist trying to show up those they called Office People, who were not real railroaders. Ralph probably saw him in particular as not just Office People but a person of no age, no experience— a child who had no business holding down a position of any authority at the Santa Fe railroad. After beginning as a clerk in the passenger traffic office, he was actually thirty-two years old and had been with the railroad for ten years. His crew-cut blond hair and baby freckled face made him seem much younger.

"I guess you'll be wanting dinner served here in the drawing room, is that right, Mr. Wheeler?" asked Ralph, as Sanders stepped back toward the door.

"That's right, Ralph. Thank you. I'll have the whitefish—

grilled—and the jellied consommé. Cold, please. That ought to do it."

"No blueberry pie tonight, sir?"

"No, no."

"Wine, sir? We're carrying a special red from France and two whites, one from—"

Wheeler's wave stopped Ralph from finishing the sentence. "Iced tea, then?"

"Just a cup of Sanka coffee, thank you."

Suddenly the Texas Chief began to move, finally showing the lighted blue circle drumhead at the rear of its observation car that had Texas Chief emblazoned on it along with an Indian chief wearing a headdress. The sign on the end of the Super Chief's observation car was similar except that its basic color was yellow.

"That's good, that's good," said Ralph. "It'll be out of our way."

Wheeler turned toward Sanders. "I hope the Santa Fe didn't bring you on this train just to see about me, Mr. Sanders."

"You and other important people aboard the Super, sir," Sanders said. "That's my wonderful job."

Otto Wheeler was not at the top of the VIP list given to Sanders for this trip, but he was on it. Seven assistant general passenger agents worked out of the Santa Fe headquarters in the Railway Exchange Building on Michigan Avenue, only a short walk north from Dearborn Station. Assisting on various publicity and travel promotion projects was their principal duty but, on occasion, they were sent off on trains with important passengers. As the junior man, Sanders caught mostly slow-train travel assignments. This was only the second time he had been on the Super Chief, which he passionately believed was the finest streamliner in the world.

"Are you ready for dinner now, sir?" Ralph asked Wheeler. "Sooner you eat, sooner I can make up your berth and all."

"Right, Ralph. I'll be ready when it's ready."

Charlie Sanders opened the drawing room door and began to exit as Ralph backed out behind him. But Wheeler said, "Could I speak with you a moment privately, Ralph?"

With smiling efficiency, Ralph motioned for Sanders to complete his departure into the passageway, then he closed the door behind him.

"Yes, sir," Ralph said to Wheeler. "What can I do for you, sir?"

"I am not able to go to the dining car, of course, but I would like to know if a particular person is there . . . a woman, dark reddish brown hair, magnificent white skin—stunningly attractive. Green eyes, a nose that is quite small. Her eyes flutter when she talks. Laughs like a . . . like she really means it. She would be traveling to Los Angeles."

"We all know her, Mr. Wheeler, and we've watched for her before many times, haven't we?"

"We have, Ralph, we surely have."

"I will find her if she's on this train tonight, Mr. Wheeler, I promise you that."

"Thank you, Ralph."

Ralph reached for the latch on the door again. "For your information, sir, there's another Super Regular, a movie man named Mr. Darwin Rinehart, in the other drawing room and a connecting bedroom here in your car. I'm sure you've seen him here on the Super before."

"Yes, yes, I have talked to him a time or two. Don't tell him I said it but his movies are mostly very awful."

Ralph smiled and said, "Here in the compartment on your other side is a Mr. Rockford, as in the town here in Illinois. Never seen him on the Super before this trip. He asked about you when he got on some thirty minutes ago or so. Wanted to know if you'd boarded yet. I thought you'd like to know who you're traveling with, sir."

"Yes, thank you, Ralph."

Ralph smiled and nodded and Wheeler returned both the smile and the nod.

"Mr. Clark Gable's with us again, too. Nobody'll probably get to see him much but I thought you'd like to know."

"Mr. Gable and I have spoken a few words back and forth here on the Super a time or two," Wheeler said. "I thought he was wonderful in *Red Hat*. So were Joan Crawford and Miss Dodsworth. Too bad that Rinehart fellow can't make movies like that."

"Yes, sir, Mr. Wheeler," said Ralph.

He had not seen *Red Hat* but he had been with Grace Dodsworth in person many times, of course, back when she was a familiar Star on the Super.

Now Ralph felt the train—*his* train—moving. As always, there was no jerking, no banging, only a gentle, majestic gliding away with a slight sound of a bell and a whistle from the engine way up front.

"We're off, Mr. Wheeler."

That first minute or so of departure was always a special time for Ralph and, it seemed to him, most everyone who ever had the supreme pleasure of departing Chicago on the greatest train in the world.

Ralph shared that joy by exchanging knowing smiles with Otto Wheeler.

But then, in a reflexive act of privacy, Ralph looked away from the tears he saw in the sick man's eyes and said farewell.

At five after nine, Ralph came to serve Clark Gable the dinner he had requested. The porter had to use his own passkey to enter the locked drawing room after getting no answer to his several knocks.

Once inside, he found Gable in a chair, sound asleep. Only one of the four bottles of scotch had been opened and it was still almost full. Ralph had known The King to routinely finish a whole bottle before dinner without showing a sign of having had a drop.

Gable was slow to rouse but before too long he was not only awake, he was alert, cutting into his sirloin steak and sipping on a glass of red wine that Ralph had set before him on a small tray table.

"Are there indeed fair prospects for the evening?" the King of Hollywood asked Ralph the porter.

"Only two worth mentioning, it seems to me," said the porter. "One a blond woman I saw first in the middle lounge below the dome car and then in the dining car. She found me and asked if I might introduce her to you, Mr. Gable. She said a couple of the others in the crew said I might be the one to help."

"How old would you say she is?" asked Gable, as if asking the size of a sport coat he was considering.

"A good thirty, maybe thirty-five, Mr. Gable."

"A looker?"

"Are there any other kind fit for The King?"

Gable, showing that smile that had helped make him famous, said, "What did you tell her?"

"Oh, the same as I tell every one of them when they ask. I told her that only The King knows where he will be and what he will do and where he will do it and what time. I assume you'll be wanting to do it at the usual time."

Clark Gable hesitated before saying, "Yes, you bet. The usual time."

"A little after ten it will be, yes, sir," said Ralph. "I will return to make up the berth in plenty of time."

"Right," said Gable. "A little after ten."

He continued with his dinner while Ralph did his chores, placing starched white sheets and fluffed pillows on the pullout divan and doing what else was necessary to get things ready for The King.

"What was the second prospect?" Gable asked Ralph.

"A brunette, also a looker, maybe slightly younger. She'd also, as I said would happen, picked up the lightning report through the train that Mr. Clark Gable was aboard tonight."

When Gable said nothing, Ralph said, "Say after eleven thirty or so for her, sir—as usual?"

"That's right—always as usual," Clark Gable said.

"Why didn't you leave that book in the compartment?" Rinehart asked.

They had already passed into the darkened Illinois countryside, the twilit sights of the railroad yards, factories, a few slums and the suburbs of Chicago now behind them.

"Because I don't want to spend my entire dinner listening to you whine about being washed up at forty because of *Dark Days*, Clark Gable's snub and all the rest," Mathews replied.

They had a large four-chair table by themselves, so arranged through Ralph by the dining car steward. There were smaller tables for two on one side of the middle aisle of the dining car, and for four on the other. Filling up the four-place tables with strangers was common practice in all railroad dining cars. It could be prevented only by eating late and/or heavily tipping all concerned. Rinehart knew and loved the ruling customs of luxury train travel.

Both he and Mathews ate the roast rib of prime beef, with the great combination salad that was a specialty of the Super Chief. It was made of ice-cold lettuce and huge slices of giant red tomatoes with a vinaigrette dressing and crumbles of blue cheese.

There was nothing to see through the windows except the flash of lights in houses and small buildings and cars and other vehicles moving along roads and highways. The moon was either not out or not bright. Rinehart, having finished his second martini and progressed well into a bottle of a nice French cabernet sauvignon, could not tell for sure where the moon was right now and was not much interested in finding out. But it triggered a thought—a very minor thought. It was based on a conversation he and Mathews had had in New York several days earlier about *Death of a Salesman*. Rinehart had been outbid five years earlier on trying to turn Arthur Miller's play into a movie.

"Miller was right," Rinehart said. "No wonder Marilyn married him."

"She married him because she was high on pills," Mathews mumbled, barely looking up from his book.

"Failure in America is too easy because success is too easy."

Mathews set the book down in his lap and gave Rinehart his full attention. "Willy Loman wasn't into stuff like that—"

"You got to make millions or win Oscars because we're a free and open country. No limit to what you can do. Be a waitress one day, a movie star the next. Be a Kansas City haberdasher one day, president the next. Anything but being on top is considered a failure because being on top is possible."

"Willy Loman never said or believed that—"

"In Russia, you finish the sixth grade, find a place to live with a bathroom, bring home a chicken, you're considered a huge success. Being on top isn't possible so not getting there isn't failure."

"So you and Willy are moving to Moscow with all the other Commies? Jesus, Dar. Before you know it, here'll come McCarthy and the Red Police." Mathews returned to his book.

Rinehart and Mathews had made this trip so many times and sat in the dining car so many evenings like this. They were somewhere in Illinois, for sure. They hadn't crossed the Mississippi yet into Iowa. That happened at Fort Madison, where the train always made a brief stop. Rinehart looked at his watch. Barely an hour out of Chicago. Still in Illinois. But *where* in Illinois?

Rinehart saw STREATOR on a station sign as the Super picked up speed. That meant Joliet was coming a few minutes later. Many movies had been set in or were about the prison in

Joliet. Just say the word *Joliet*, and people think of electric chairs and crying families of death row inmates.

"What about a television series set on death row in a prison?" Rinehart asked Mathews, who did a double take, grinned for the first time in weeks and then closed his book and set it down. Both of them had already finished their dessert, warm apple pie with a slice of cheddar cheese melted on top and a dollop of vanilla ice cream on the side.

"You serious, Dar? You really thinking about doing television? That is great. If I was still drinking I would set 'em up for the house."

He had another sip of his Coke and Rinehart took a gulp of red wine.

Rinehart said, "Yeah, yeah. Let's play it out, Gene. We'll call it *Joliet*. Each week an inmate is electrocuted. That would be the pitch . . ."

"Right, right," said Mathews. "Every Thursday night at nine, right here on NBC—or whatever—come watch a heinous criminal get executed!"

"There'd be the ongoing cast of a warden, a priest, some guards, reporters and the entire population on death row that always has new people coming in to take the places of those executed . . ."

"We could maybe get big-name guest stars to come on each week and take the juice. Some could get fried for murder, some for treason, some for rape . . ."

Here they were, like old times, playing it out.

Rinehart said, "There'd be flashbacks to their crimes, lots of tears from their victims and loved ones . . ."

Mathews said, "We'd ask Clark Gable, The King himself, to guest star. He'd make a spectacular electrocuted corpse, don't you think?"

"I can smell him now . . ."

"Maybe one week we'd have an attempted prison breakout from death row. Maybe even one that was successful. An innocent man gets out to prove his innocence . . ."

Back and forth they went, the way they always did.

"Or a guilty one gets out to kill the prosecutor who sent him to death row . . ."

"One week, the warden could start sleeping with one of the death row inmates' visiting wives. Maybe knock her up . . ."

"The baby could be brought up in the prison nursery by a convicted murderess with a heart of gold . . ."

"Every once in a while a convict would be proved innocent seconds before the switch was to be thrown. That would be where the reporter characters would come in. Heroes all, of course—"

"Of course. We'd go into detail about last meals, last requests, last statements, last-minute confessions, last sex, last fantasies . . ."

"Shoot the whole thing right there in the prison at Joliet. Think of the great publicity that'd be for the great State of Illinois . . ."

"I'm not sure we could get Loretta Young or one of her TV types to go for it but who knows?"

When they finished, she was the first to speak.

"You really are The King . . . Mr. Gable," she said.

Gable did not say thank you or anything else, expressing whatever he had to say with a pleasant grunt as he, in several quick moves, pushed away from her, swung his legs down from the bed, stood up and pulled up his dark red silk pajama bottoms.

"I remember that chest from *It Happened One Night*," she said. "But it didn't have any hair on it in the movie, like it does now."

"I let it grow out," he said. The subject clearly annoyed him.

She just laughed. Then she said, "I just have to know. One of those awful movie magazines wrote that Claudette Colbert is a . . . you know, a lady queer. That can't be true, can it?"

Gable shrugged. He was now standing with his back to her, seemingly looking for something.

"I'll bet you don't even remember *my* name, do you?" she asked.

Turning to face her, he said, "Betty?"

"No. It's Sarah."

"Same thing," he said.

She started to laugh but caught herself. It was clear he was not joking. He meant what he said.

Clark Gable had found what he was looking for. He held her two light nylon stockings in one hand and her bright pink panties in the other.

She paid no attention to that and made no move to get out of bed. She said, "I am Sarah Strother and I live in Jefferson City, Missouri. I'm going to get off in Kansas City and take an early-morning Missouri Pacific on home. My husband is a lawyer and I work for the lieutenant governor of Missouri as his legislative assistant. He's a Democrat. What are you?"

"A Republican," said Gable.

"Why?"

"I was in the war with Ike."

"Everyone who was in the war was in it with Ike."

Now Gable extended and raised his arms, offering the woman her stockings and panties. "I think it's time for both of us to get some sleep," he said. "I'm going to need that entire bed, small as it is."

She pulled the sheet and blanket away from her and scooted to the edge of the bed. Her eyes remained fixed on Gable.

"Your ears really aren't that big, Mr. Gable," she said. "I hate what they say about your ears."

Gable's friendly smile disappeared.

"Well, whatever, I still can't believe this happened," she

said. Still naked, she stood up. "I have never ever played around on my husband. Never ever. Maybe if I told him it was with Clark Gable he wouldn't mind."

Gable was shaking his head as he handed her the panties.

"Don't tell him?" she said, taking the stockings and then reaching for her bra and then her slip and the rest of her clothes.

"I wouldn't, if I were you," Gable said, barely paying attention as she dressed. "Husbands don't like to hear stuff like that from their wives, no matter who was involved. In fact, doing it with somebody like me might even make it worse."

Dressed, she took a step to be in front of the tiny mirror over the small stainless steel washbasin in one corner of the drawing room.

"I don't even want to comb my hair or change anything about the way I look . . . you know, after it was over. This was kind of an historic thing for me."

Gable said nothing.

She turned toward him one last time but made no effort to kiss him good-bye or even to touch him. She clearly knew for sure what had happened was now over.

"Can I ask you one last favor before I go, Mr. Gable?"

Gable gave her a smile. It contained the answer—depends on what the favor is.

"Would you say *it* for me?"

He didn't have to ask what *it* was.

Accompanied by a fulsome grin, he said, " 'Frankly, my dear, I don't give a damn.' "

She giggled and clutched her arms across her chest. "I didn't even notice your false teeth the movie magazines write about so much," she said.

Those were her last words as she left the presence of The King.

Rinehart and Mathews encountered Ralph standing in the narrow passageway. They were heading back from the dining car; he was knocking on a compartment door with one hand, holding a tray of food in the other.

"Sounds like a secret signal of some kind." Mathews laughed. "One long, two shorts?"

Ralph, who hadn't seen the two Hollywood Regulars coming, jumped away from the door as if he'd been shot at. "No, sir, just bringing a passenger a late-night snack . . ."

At that moment, the bedroom door opened. And there stood Ralph's Private.

Rinehart and then Mathews glanced at the man as they squeezed by Ralph.

Neither looked back as Ralph took the tray on into the bedroom and closed the door behind him.

"There was something familiar about that guy," Rinehart said.

"Not to me . . . well, now that you mention it, maybe so," Mathews said. "A movie type—a bit actor?"

Rinehart shook his head. "I don't think so. Maybe he's from the news. Maybe his picture was in the paper."

"What kind of news?"

"The government kind . . . Washington probably," said Rinehart. "I'll think of it eventually. I know faces. Remember Tracy Thurber?"

Tracy Thurber was a beautiful twenty-four-year-old junior high school English teacher who was discovered by Rinehart while she was riding on a trolley in downtown Los Angeles. Rinehart saw her face in the trolley window, ran after her to the next car stop and, on the spot, offered her a part in his upcoming movie *Dark Days*.

She spent fifteen days with Rinehart, Mathews and the crew shooting on location in Utah.

"Excuse me, Mr. Rinehart," said Charlie Sanders as he slipped into a seat across from Darwin Rinehart in the darkened observation car lounge.

It was almost midnight, an hour into Iowa after crossing the Mississippi River at Fort Madison. The Texas Chief had stayed far enough ahead so the Super Chief was on time, in keeping with what Santa Fe advertising called The Chief Way.

Charlie introduced himself and said, "I am a huge fan of the movies, sir. I would say that I am more than just a fan, actually, I am a student of the movies."

Rinehart looked only at the glass of scotch in front of him. "I love movies, sir. I really do."

Rinehart kept his look downward.

"I have an idea for a movie, sir. That's why I am talking . . ."

"Everybody has an idea for a movie, kid. No offense—but go away, please. I like to be alone in here." Rinehart spoke quietly but firmly and still without paying any real attention to Charlie Sanders.

Sanders knew all about Rinehart and his traveling habits. He had read in a movie magazine—one of several he bought reguarly—that Rinehart preferred to sip scotch by himself in the rear lounge late into the night after having dinner in the dining car with his longtime associate Gene Mathews.

There was now, in fact, no other person in the car—not even a bartender or steward, unless one was sleeping back there in the dark somewhere. They often did while off duty. The only light came from a small art deco lamp between Sanders and Rinehart.

"My movie idea, the whole movie from beginning to end, takes place here—on the Super Chief, sir."

There, he had done it. Charlie Sanders, on behalf of the Santa Fe, had had such an idea for a while—all part of his natural thinking of movies as a way to promote travel The Chief Way. On assignment now and thus required to stay awake and on the job, he let his mind rest and linger on the fact that this was indeed the Train of the Stars. And this very night there was not only Clark Gable on board but also, Sanders knew, Darwin Rinehart, who had much experience with train movies.

"Sorry, kid, I know you mean well for your railroad but we have rules in the business about talking to people about their ideas. You talk, I listen, I make a picture, you claim I stole your idea, you sue me. Besides, they already did that picture four years ago."

"Yes, sir. Gloria Swanson starred in it. *Three For Bedroom C* it was called."

"Yeah. She loved the Super so much she had her studio make it solely on her clout from *Sunset Boulevard*. Big mistake for her and everybody involved. Lousy idea, lousy movie. It stank all the way from LA to Chicago and back ten times. End of discussion."

"What if it starred Claudette Colbert?" Sanders said.

"Too French—too foreigny."

Sanders, the big movies student, wanted to blast back in fierce defense of Claudette Colbert, who he believed was one of Hollywood's best actresses. But that would have sidetracked his mission of the moment. "What about *Silver Streak*?" he asked.

Rinehart set his drink down hard on the table and smiled. "You know about *Silver Streak*, kid?"

"Yes, sir. It came out in 1934 . . ."

Rinehart held up his right hand. Shut up, kid, was the message. "That was the first picture I ever worked on. I was just a kid myself. I had a tall hill of hair on my head then. Came down to Hollywood from Sacramento. An uncle knew the producer, a helluva guy named Allvine—Glendon Allvine. He hired me to be a gofer. I got coffee and ran errands and got my feet wet in the picture business. We made some of it around here somewhere . . ."

"Galesburg, Illinois. Yes, sir. The Super Chief passed through there earlier tonight—as I'm sure you, a prominent Super Regular, know. Most of the action shots for *Silver Streak* with the Burlington Zephyr were taken there, weren't they?"

"Yeah, that's right. How come you know so much about this?"

Charlie Sanders only grinned. Knowing this kind of stuff had been his passion since he was a *real* kid going to movies in the Chicago suburb of Garrison, Indiana. Now, for the Santa Fe, it was his business to know it.

Rinehart spoke softly, almost to the darkness rather than Charlie, as he had earlier to the Chicago suburbs.

"Allvine talked the Burlington into loaning us their new silver streamliner train. It was the first diesel like that. What a time we had. There were no stars. Sally Blane and Charles Starrett played the leads. Nobody's heard of them before or since. Sally Blane was Loretta Young's sister in real life. That silver train was the real star of the picture—"

"Yes, sir, and this one could be one again."

"—No budget. Allvine made that for less than a hundred thousand dollars real money. Amazing, truly amazing. The story wasn't much either. Something about an iron lung."

"Yes, sir. They used the new streamliner to race an iron lung from Chicago to a sick man at Boulder Dam outside Las

Vegas in Nevada. The sick man was the son of the owner of the railroad and the brother of the girl who was in love with the scientist designer who invented the diesel streamliner train—"

"Corny idea, corny everything but it was the first picture about the new streamliners and it made a lot of money for the company that is now called RKO. Great shots at Boulder Dam, too. They were still building some of it at the time. How do you know so much about this picture, kid? Most people never heard of it."

"I saw it at college in a public relations class on how to do company publicity. Burlington got a lot of great free publicity out of that movie."

Sanders, even in the faint light, could see pleasure in Rinehart's face.

"I've also read the book about the movie—it had the script and little essays by the producer, director, even the sound man about making the movie," said Charlie, pressing his advantage.

"Yeah, yeah. I remember that. I have a copy of the book myself somewhere. It came out the next year."

"There was also a *Silver Streak* Big Little Books for kids that was published at the same time."

Darwin Rinehart took a long, long sip of his scotch. "Beginnings and endings," he sighed to Sanders and everyone else in the world. "*Silver Streak* was my beginning."

"The Super Chief would be a natural, great, fantastic next chapter," said Sanders.

"More like an ending, I'd say."

"I guess I ought to go, sir. I'm sorry I bothered you." Sanders made a slight move to stand.

Darwin Rinehart told him to stay where he was.

"Go ahead. What's your Super Chief idea, kid?"

Charlie Sanders had, by now, gotten used to being called kid by this movie man despite the fact that, according to the movie magazines, Rinehart himself was forty—only eight years older than this Santa Fe man.

"I can't think of anything else . . . you know . . . that I can do to help you . . . you know, get extended," said the brunette, Fair Visitor #2.

"I know, I know," said Clark Gable. He was upset—embarrassed. "I think you should put on your clothes and leave."

The woman, as Ralph had advertised, was a brunette and slightly younger than #1, but she was as pretty and had about the same proportions.

"One more try, please?" she asked.

"It's not going to do any good. Please go."

Gable rolled out of the berth and she followed him. Both were naked. Soon he had put his pajama bottoms back on and she was back into her two-piece dark blue traveling suit.

She moved toward the door, stopped and then burst into tears.

Gable made a leaning motion to go to her and maybe even to put an arm around her shoulders. But he didn't. "What's the problem?" he asked.

"I can't believe this," she said through her sobs. "I'm with Clark Gable, the sexiest man on the face of the earth, and I can't . . . you know, arouse him."

"It's not you," said Gable.

She pulled away from him, the tears having slightly moderated. "I read a story in *Confidential* magazine about your having five, six, even seven women a night. It just *has* to be me." She began crying again.

Gable went to the pockets of his sport coat, which was hanging on a hook nearby. "Here, take this," he said, handing her a ten-dollar bill.

She grabbed the bill, crushed it in her hand and threw it back at him. It struck his chest and fell to the floor. "I'm an English teacher. I teach the seventh grade. I did this for the occasion, for history—not money!" she shouted.

Gable put a finger to his lips. "Let's hold it down, all right?"

Then, suddenly, the woman's eyes were no longer teary. They were squinting with wisdom—revelation. "You can't be a pansy like I read in *Confidential* Van Johnson was, can you, Clark Gable? Not you, The King of sex?" There was as much accusation as question in the words.

Gable handed her another ten-dollar bill. "No, no. I'm just tired. I just couldn't . . . do it. Not again. You were the twelfth girl I've had this evening."

She took the money this time and slammed the door behind her as she left the compartment.

"It's to remake *Silver Streak* for today, right now in the fifties," said Charlie Sanders. "That's my idea."

"Forget it," said Darwin Rinehart. "They don't use iron lungs anymore for polio. They give shots. Salk vaccine kind of shots."

"I know. It has to be something else besides an iron lung."

"Forget it. Now trains are for people like me who prefer and can afford slow, easy traveling, not rush emergencies. They're losing their business to cars and airplanes. Trains are on the way out except for a few of us. Forget it."

"Some people are afraid to fly. Instead of an iron lung that is rushed west on the train it could be a person. But it could still follow a lot of the same things that happened in *Silver Streak*. We could have a bad guy, like they did, who tries to sabotage the Super Chief."

Rinehart's eyes were closed. Sanders couldn't tell if the scotch and whatever else he'd consumed was the cause or he was simply deep in thought about a Super Chief movie.

Charlie Sanders pushed on. "The president of Burlington, as a public relations move, loaned out his new train for the movie. I know we at the Santa Fe would do the same thing with the Super Chief. I just know we would."

Without appearing to open his eyes, Rinehart said, in a near whisper: "We shot most of the railroad shots with the Zephyr at that town in Illinois . . . what was it?"

"Galesburg," said Sanders.

"Yeah. At the studio in Hollywood we did a 'clinch' shot with Blane and Starrett, the lovebirds. We even had a phony diesel engine the studio made as a prop."

"I think I read that the whole idea for the movie came from a man who was editor of a magazine called *Diesel Digest*. He fought his way in to see Allvine and sold him on the idea. It's not that different from what I'm trying to do now, sir. Here I am, Sanders of the Santa Fe, making a pitch to the great Darwin Rinehart."

"Yeah, yeah." Rinehart had opened his eyes. And he was smiling. "But this isn't how we do it. Our movies come from books. I don't read books for picture ideas. Gene does that for me. Then somebody comes in and does The Talk about the picture that could be made from the book. Do me a talk if you can, kid."

Darwin Rinehart glanced out the window at the lights of small towns and farmland and then said, "But make it snappy. It's already past midnight."

"Yes, sir!"

But before Charlie Sanders could start, Rinehart said: "What about Joliet? Did we go through Joliet, Illinois?"

"Yes, sir. That was before Galesburg."

"Good, good. Okay, kid, you're on."

Fair Visitor #2 had been gone from Clark Gable's drawing room only a few moments when Ralph reappeared.

"Just wanted to see if there was anything else I could get you tonight, sir."

Gable grinned. "Nope. I've had more than I can handle for one night."

"Yes, sir," said Ralph. "I assume you'll be wanting a shave in the morning in the barber shop, as usual?"

Gable frowned. "No, no. I'll shave myself."

"That'll disappoint Mr. Josephs for sure."

Gable was still frowning. "Mr. Josephs?"

"He's a substitute barber on this run. Normally, he does the Chief or the Texas Chief. Your regulars are all either on vacation or on other trains. Mr. Josephs was looking forward to shaving The King for the first time in his barber's life."

The frown disappeared. Gable said, "I've never seen him before? He's never shaved me before in his life?"

"That's right."

"Well, then, let's not disappoint him. Make me an appointment."

"Usual time, sir?"

"What times does he have open?"

"Any time is always open for you, Mr. Gable. I already told him eight thirty, your usual time."

"Certainly. The usual. Eight thirty it is."

"When would you like to begin with the Fair Visitors today, sir?" asked Ralph. "There are several waiting notification—one or two, I believe, will be leaving the train fairly early in the day . . ."

Gable held up his right hand, palm out. "I think we'll hold off on that—for now, at least," he said. "I'm feeling a bit weary."

Ralph smiled, nodded his head as if to royalty and left.

Charlie Sanders, talking as snappily as he ever had in his life, just made it up off the top of his head. It was already late and he knew Darwin Rinehart was not going to give him much time.

"A pretty young woman is dying in Albuquerque. She has a serious brain disorder that can only be cured and her life saved by one man—a handsome young brain surgeon who has the perfect set of hands for the delicate operation it will take. He is known as the best in the world for this particular operation. Usually people come to him but the Albuquerque woman is too sick to travel. So he must come to her."

"Where does he live?" Rinehart asked.

"How about Galesburg, Illinois, because of the *Silver Streak* connection?"

"Nobody lives in Galesburg, Illinois."

"Carl Sandburg did."

"My point exactly. Put him in Kansas City."

"Done. Yes, sir. The surgeon's in Kansas City. We get there in less than three hours, in fact—you know, tonight here on the Super Chief."

Rinehart said, "Yes, I know. That's why I thought of it. Of course, nothing ever happens in Kansas City either except in *Oklahoma!*—the movie—when that dancer did a song about it being up-to-date."

"Wasn't that Gene Nelson?"

"Right, right. Lee Dixon played the part on Broadway. Rod Steiger stole the movie playing Jud Fry. Nobody ever dreamed he could sing. You wake him up in the middle of the night and I'll bet he's still Jud Fry. Actors are the characters they play forever."

Rinehart must have seen a look of disbelief on Sanders's face because he quickly added:

"Hey, kid, I was at a dinner party one night in Beverly Hills. A guy had a heart attack sitting right there at the table. Lew Ayres, without saying a word, got down on the floor with the man, did a lot of doctor things and saved his life. He did it on reflex—instinct. Back in the thirties and forties he'd played Dr. Jimmy Kildare in nine pictures for MGM. Once a doctor in a movie, always a doctor. Once a pig man in *Oklahoma!*, always a pig man. That's it."

Then he looked at his wristwatch, nodded, signaling to the kid to return to The Talk—and make it snappy.

"Well . . . the surgeon's afraid to fly," said Sanders. "He's been on one airplane and he almost died of a nervous break-down. He vomited and cried like a baby—"

"I don't do vomit pictures."

"Yes, sir. The important thing is that he won't fly anymore and that means he has to take the Super Chief to the sick woman in Albuquerque, who he saves and then falls in love with and then marries—"

"The surgeon's the hero of the picture?"

"Yes, sir."

"Heroes can't be afraid. Not in the movies. Got to be an-other reason he won't fly and why he's on the Super Chief. You also got to have things happen on the train—a little murder, romance, maybe have a spy like they did in the first *Silver Streak*. Nothing much ever happens on trains in real life any-more except eating, drinking and sex so you'd have to make it up. This train, the best in the world, is half empty right now on this trip. Nothing's happening on it. Right now I'm going to bed."

Sanders stood with Darwin Rinehart. "I have to remain on duty, sir."

Rinehart blinked, frowned. "What's there to do in the mid-dle of the night for an assistant whatever kind of agent you said you were?"

"We have a really special passenger coming aboard in Kansas City," said Sanders with a tone of pride. "I must be ready."

Rinehart knew the world of the Super Chief. It would not stop at Kansas City until two thirty in the morning. There, some of the cars would be temporarily separated from the rest of the train so another sleeper coach could be inserted. Passengers could board that car in Kansas City after nine o'clock the night before, bed down in their compartment and be fast asleep by the time the Super Chief itself actually arrived at Kansas City's Union Station.

"Who is the special passenger—a surgeon with special hands?" said Rinehart.

"Can't say, sir," Charlie Sanders said, stiffly. This was no joking matter. "All I can say is that I will be assisted in my duties by a special agent of the Santa Fe Railway Police."

Darwin Rinehart gave a halfhearted mocking whistle. Big deal!

"He'll be in plainclothes—like me," Sanders added. "So you might not know when he's there."

Rinehart gave a second whistle.

Jack Pryor was that Santa Fe police detective. He still had the build and moves of the six-foot/205-pound fullback he had been in high school.

"Mr. Truman told me he's a light sleeper," Pryor said to Charlie Sanders, who at five nine/160 pounds had played only second-string baseball in high school. "I hope all this noise of the switching didn't wake him up. He was here right at nine o'clock as soon as the Kansas City sleeper was ready for passengers."

The two Santa Fe men, having met and joined forces, were talking at trainside there at the Union Station platform, where the outside clocks now showed the time to be two thirty-five in the morning.

"What'll we do if he gets up and starts walking around the train?" Sanders asked.

"I'll protect him, you entertain him—isn't that what we're here to do?"

"Did you like Truman—you know, as president?" asked Sanders.

"You bet. He dropped the bomb and stopped the war. I was only an MP in San Francisco," said Pryor, a tall, stocky, black-haired man in his fifties. "But what he did kept me from getting any closer to the hot stuff. You're a Korea vet, aren't you?"

"Kind of," said Sanders. "I joined the Air Force to be a pilot but washed out of flight school and ended up teaching communications at an air base in San Antonio."

"We were both lucky."

Pryor and Sanders had worked together a couple of times and mostly liked each other, but their difference in age kept them from being really close. There was also a touch of a class problem. Pryor had only a high school education; Sanders was a business administration graduate of the University of Indiana at Bloomington. That aside, Pryor, with body language as well as words, always let it be known in a friendly manner that, whatever they were doing, he was the senior man present.

"What about Mrs. Truman?" Sanders asked.

"She's not with him. He said she came down with a cold at the last minute and stayed home."

"Good, good. Only one of them to worry about."

"Anybody else special who is already on the train that I should know about?" Pryor asked.

"Only Clark Gable. Is everything they say about him true?"

"If your question has to do with women and drinking on the Super Chief, it is," Pryor said.

That was exactly what Sanders had in mind with his question.

"There's also a movie producer named Rinehart aboard. He's in one of the observation car drawing rooms. He's a Regular. I talked to him about making a movie aboard the Super. That's the kind of work I do for the good of the railroad. Mr. Wheeler's in the other drawing room. You know him?"

"Everybody who knows the Super knows him," Pryor said. "I'll bet he spends more time on this train than most of the crew."

"He's really ill . . ."

Then it happened. Charlie Sanders grabbed Pryor's right arm and pointed him toward the front of the train. "My God, look who's coming."

Pryor immediately recognized the man walking toward them. It was Clark Gable. Who wouldn't know that look—that presence? He was in dark gray suit pants and an unbuttoned white dress shirt with a big collar but no tie. His black shoes shined like mirrors.

"Good morning, Mr. Gable," Pryor said when Gable got to them. "Welcome to Kansas City."

"Morning," said Gable, smiling. He was puffing on a cigarette. "Couldn't sleep. Thought I'd stretch my legs a bit."

"That's great, Mr. Gable," said Sanders nervously. "I'm an assistant general passenger agent with the Santa Fe. Are you getting everything you need here on the Super Chief, sir? If there's anything you need I will be available on the train. Just ask your porter or one of the conductors to find me."

Clark Gable's smile broadened. "I'm getting more than everything I need. Thanks."

"I'm Jack Pryor, a special agent of the Santa Fe police, Mr. Gable."

"Nice to meet you both," said Gable. "I guess I'd better start back toward my car. Wouldn't want to be left in Kansas City."

He laughed. Sanders and Pryor laughed.

Clark Gable raised his hand in the form of a salute as he walked away.

Sanders and Pryor watched him from the rear in silence.

"Wow," said Sanders. "Thank you, Mr. Santa Fe Railway, for making that possible in my life."

Pryor said, "He seemed smaller than I expected. Shorter, thinner."

"Movies make everything and everybody look bigger than they really are, I guess," Sanders said.

They started moving toward the train.

Sanders said, "They told me in Chicago that we're making a quick, off-the-books stop in Strong for somebody else who's important—important to our railroad, at least."

A conductor yelled "All aboard!" And then so did another farther up.

Sanders jumped on the train after Pryor and within a minute the Super Chief was moving again.

Darwin Rinehart, after so many trips, still saw his drawing room as being exquisite, ideally fit for kings, particularly when the connecting bedroom was added into the mix. Gene Mathews was in the bedroom, no doubt fast asleep.

It was so much more than the space.

Small lamps on the walls between the windows in Rinehart's drawing room were lit just enough to show the soft pastel colors of light blue, green and sandy brown on the window shades, carpet, chairs, wood paneling and ceiling.

The bed was made up and ready for him, its crisp white sheets and blue blanket turned down and gleaming.

There was a smell of soap, varnish, chrome—cleanliness, spic, span, class.

Rinehart leaned down, pulled a blind and looked out the

large window into the darkness. It was after midnight; the Super Chief was zipping through another small town. He yanked the blind back down and quickly removed his clothes, hung them in a small closet, dressed in a pair of light blue silk pajamas and lay down.

The Super Chief. He was on the Super Chief. He was lying down in a drawing room on the Super Chief, the greatest train in America, on its way to Los Angeles, California, and the Pacific Ocean. The Super Chief. Thirty-nine and one-quarter hours was all it took for its streak across the American heartland. Yes, a *silver* streak. A nine-car streak of silver luxury behind a magnificent diesel engine painted in the Santa Fe's famous red and yellow "Warbonnet" colors.

Rinehart heard and felt the clicking of the wheels on the track. And there was an occasional *Whaaa!* blast from the train's horn as it zipped through the dark Missouri countryside. It had the sound of a howl—more like an animal than a machine.

That's because this train is alive, thought Rinehart. Maybe the Santa Fe kid's right about making a movie that takes place on this wonderful train.

He felt a moment's curiosity about who the special passenger might be who was boarding there and stayed wide awake with his own thoughts about what this particular trip on the Super might mean for his own failed life.

And then he felt the train slowing down and he listened and tossed with it as it came to a full stop at Kansas City's Union Station. There came the banging as the cars were switched around.

And he wondered again about the famous person who was joining the Super Chief now.

He couldn't resist raising the window blind.

There was nothing to see except a well-lit platform and one or two porters and conductors walking around, talking.

Then he saw two men, dressed in regular civilian suits with ties and felt hats, standing off to the right. One of them was that Santa Fe kid. Maybe the other was the railroad cop he was talking about?

A third man came up to them. He was smoking a cigarette. There was something familiar about the guy. Heavy black hair, neatly combed straight back, graying sideburns, a slight mustache . . .

Oh, sure. It was just Clark Gable.

Rinehart wanted to yell through the window at Gable. Tell him how he shouldn't have treated him, Darwin Rinehart, like he was a loser. *You'd be nowhere without* Gone with the Wind*!*

But he just watched as Gable, after exchanging a few words with the other two men, disappeared up toward the rear end of the train.

Rinehart pulled the blind back down and closed his eyes. He still had no idea about who the special passenger was in a compartment in the Kansas City sleeping car.

Or what he was going to do with the rest of his life.

He finally dozed off after going through several possible titles for a movie that takes place entirely on the Super Chief.

As the Super glided away from Kansas City, Dale Lawrence, the disheveled Private, sat staring out the window at the dark, his bleary eyes popped opened, his cough erupting.

For a few precious minutes he had violated the porter's orders not to leave the roomette. That was when he went across the passageway to the other side of the train so he could see the Kansas City station's platform.

He moved finally into the vestibule between his car and the one behind where he could also hear.

He watched carefully as the two men in suits and hats talked and then greeted another man, who seemed familiar. Lawrence thought he resembled Clark Gable.

But that was of no serious interest. What he overheard in a conversation between a porter and a conductor, about Harry S Truman now being on the train, was what was important.

That was all that mattered to Dale L. Lawrence.

Gene Mathews considered himself the champion train sleeper. He had yet to meet anyone who claimed the ability to doze off as quickly as he could to the sounds and swings of a sleeping car berth. Over the many years and trips with Darwin Rinehart, he had developed an almost hypnotic heavy-lid response to putting his head down on a pillow and closing his eyes on a moving train.

He was asleep but he was also aware of what was happening. The *click-click-click* of the wheels passing over the tracks reminded him of the gadget, called a metronome, his little sister used when practicing the piano. She'd wind it up and a skinny metal stem would tick side to side, side to side. Gene could also hear the *ding-ding* of the downed barriers at railroad crossings and even, faintly, the occasional blast of the Super Chief's horn from the engine far ahead of him, here in the observation car at the end of the train.

He heard it all and yet he heard nothing that roused him completely. The commotion of Kansas City had barely stirred him because it, too, was built into his unconscious expectation of the first night out on the Super from Chicago.

But now, suddenly, he was awake. Sitting up.

There had been an abrupt, noticeable change in the click-click rhythm.

Mathews was certain they couldn't have been much more than an hour out of Kansas City. It was too early for Bethel . . .

The train came to a full stop.

He raised his window blind.

There was a small red brick train station. Only a few lights were on inside and out. A rectacular black and white sign on the building showed the word s-t-r-o-n-g. Strong, Kansas? Gene knew the entire timetable of the Super Chief. It definitely did not have a scheduled stop in Strong.

Strong, Kansas. There was something familiar about it, though. Didn't somebody famous live here? Not a movie person. There actually were a *few* famous people who weren't in the movies.

Yes! It was an editor. A writer. Albert Roland Browne. Gene had read a couple of his short stories. And was it him or his brother or a son who wrote the book that the movie *My Son Greg* was based on?

But it didn't matter.

The Super Chief was moving again. Whatever the reason for stopping in Albert Roland Browne's hometown, it wasn't for more than a couple of minutes.

And soon Mathews was back to sleep.

He might peer out again at Bethel. There was never much to see there but it was a scheduled crew change stop, and new passengers were permitted to board if they were going to Albuquerque or beyond.

Gene Mathews knew the Super.

And he knew he was going to miss it almost as much as Darwin Rinehart would.

A portly man in his fifties wearing a French-cuffed white shirt with large silver and pearl cuff links and a dark green tie entered the unlit interior of the empty observation car lounge. Under his right arm was a black portable Royal typewriter; in his left hand, a jumble of papers.

He went directly to the writing table just inside the car, made his writing equipment and himself comfortable, placed a monocle in his right eye, switched on a lamp and started typing.

In less than five minutes, the door opened again and three men, walking single file, came in. All three were in suits, ties. The last, the oldest, wore wire-rimmed glasses and walked with a stick.

The man at the desk stopped typing, glanced up and then leapt to his feet. To the elderly man, he said, "Are you who I think you are . . . sir?"

"I don't know who you had in mind but I'm Harry Truman of Independence, Missouri," said Truman, extending his right hand.

"That's exactly who I had in mind. I'm A. C. Browne of the *Strong*, Kansas, *Pantagraph*," said Browne as he shook hands. He did so with a manner that he hoped showed he was somewhat at ease in the company of a former president of the United States.

"You any kin to that famous Albert Roland Browne . . . what did they call him?"

"The Sage of Strong," said Browne. "He was my father. I took over the paper from him. I'm Albert *Carlton* Browne. Everybody calls me A.C."

Truman peered hard through the semidarkness. "That

fancy tie and shirt and that accent of yours look and sound more Britain and London than Kansas and Strong."

A. C. Browne was flustered. But the lack of good light helped him cover it. "I guess I picked up some habits while in Britain with NBC during the war," he said, still sounding non-Kansan.

"Well, like they say," said Truman, "You can take the man out of NBC but you can't take NBC out of the man."

Browne laughed. He could think of no other reaction.

Truman said, moving on, "These are Santa Fe people." He motioned toward the men who had preceded him into the car and were now standing poised a few feet away.

"This one's a detective. His name is Pryor. He was put here by the railroad to make sure nobody harms this tired old body of mine."

Then with a nod to the other man, the youngest of the three, Truman added, "This is Charlie. He's from the Chicago head office. He was put here by the mighty Santa Fe to make sure my every need is met, including that for a glass of whiskey in the middle of the night, even if we're in a dry state."

"Which Kansas certainly is, Mr. Truman," said Browne. "The driest of the driest."

Charlie Sanders held up a tiny key. "Coming right up, Mr. President. The steward awarded me the key to the liquor cabinet."

"You want to join me in a drink, Mr. Browne?" Truman said.

"Simple gin in a simple glass would be great, yes, sir."

Browne then followed Truman to two seats farther into the

lounge. Jack Pryor, on his way with Charlie Sanders to the liquor, switched on a light for them.

Once seated, Browne said to Truman, "This is quite an honor, sir. Thank you."

Truman nodded.

"Actually, you and I have met before, Mr. President."

"Is that right? Refresh me on that, please."

"I interviewed you in the White House in 1949 for *Look* magazine."

Charlie Sanders returned with the drinks and handed one each to Truman and to Browne. Then he disappeared into the out-of-hearing darkness with Pryor. They would watch but not listen to Harry Truman of Independence and A. C. Browne of Strong have a drink together.

Truman gave Browne a hard look. "Oh, yes, yes. I remember you. You're the one who also wrote a book about adopting a war orphan."

"Yes, sir, *My Son Greg*," said Browne, nodding. "It was based on the adoption of my real son—his name is Bart, as in Hobart."

"I didn't realize it was a true story, Browne. Good for you. Mrs. Truman and I saw the movie. Robert Taylor was in it. And that child actress?"

"Betsy Randolph."

"That's her. Is she still in the movies?"

"I don't know, sir. The porter told me there are, as always, movie stars and movie moguls on this train. We could ask one of them."

" 'The Train of the Stars' is what they've always called the Super Chief. Who are the stars this time?"

"Clark Gable's the only one I know for sure. Some travel under phony names—and the Santa Fe people keep their secret."

"We had one of those stars come to the White House who'd played a bit part as Ulysses S. Grant in some damned movie. He went into his Grant personality—I think he was drunk, too, just like Grant—and started lecturing me on how I could have won the war without dropping the bomb. I reminded him that playing smart people in the movies doesn't make you smart. He didn't like it. He did finally shut up but not before accidentally calling me 'Mr. Lincoln' a time or two."

Browne chuckled as he tried, in vain, to think of who that actor might have been. He couldn't remember ever seeing Grant portrayed by anyone in a movie. But Browne had been around enough actors and actresses to know that some of them never got over being the parts they played.

Truman took a sip of his whiskey and added, "But I must say, Browne, that the way things are going in this country it wouldn't surprise me if one of them ends up in the Senate or the House—maybe even the White House—someday."

"That'll never happen, sir."

"That's what they said about cars and diesel locomotives and airplanes. Never happen, never happen. Let's not forget our current president—my beloved successor."

"Ike?"

"He was just a general before he was a president. MacArthur got where he did only because he was more of an actor than a soldier."

"But is that fair, to lump Eisenhower with MacArthur?"

"Who gives a damn what's fair at four thirty in the morning in the lounge car on the Super Chief?"

"I'll drink to that," Browne said.

They clinked their glasses.

"What are you doing up this late, anyhow, Browne?" Truman asked.

"I just got on the train, sir. I dropped my baggage and my suit coat in my compartment and came on down here. It was empty until you got here. What about you, Mr. President?"

"I had been asleep in my compartment, but the banging of my car in Kansas City a while ago woke me up. So I decided to get up and find me a drink. Where did you get on?"

"Strong."

"I wondered about that stop. I thought the Super Chief didn't stop in Strong—or anywhere else much between Kansas City and Albuquerque."

"It did tonight, sir."

"For you?"

Browne lifted his glass and took a long sip of gin.

"You must be a Republican," Truman said.

"All I did was make a call to an old Santa Fe friend of the

family who had the Super Chief stop for me. I jumped on, the train wasn't still more than a minute or two. Why are you going to Los Angeles, sir—I assume that's your destination?"

"To make a political speech for an old friend. You?"

"To interview some folks for a magazine story I'm writing."

"You're a real chip off the father's block, aren't you?"

"Not really, sir. He didn't drink, I do. He didn't smoke, I do. He didn't cuss, I do."

"You must be a Democrat."

"I did support you and Roosevelt."

Truman smiled and grumbled something under his breath about 1948 when it was Truman and Barkley. Then he said, "Your Kansas fella Landon lost even bigger to FDR than the experts said I was going to lose to Dewey. I got to know Landon. He's a good man . . ." He stopped in midsentence. "Did you hear that?" he asked Browne.

"What, sir?"

"That *pow!* sound."

"All I heard was this train beginning to slow down."

Truman looked out the window. Some early signs of light were coming up from the bottom of the darkness over central Kansas.

"Bethel's coming up in a few minutes," said Browne. "Just a short stop here for a crew change and to put on some galley supplies. The Fred Harvey people run a farm outside town where they raise their produce and other staples for the trains and Harvey House restaurants along the Santa Fe. They've got a big laundry here, too. We did a story about it in the *Pantagraph* a while ago—"

"Detective Pryor! Detective Pryor!" Ralph, the sleeping car porter, came running into the lounge.

"Conductor Hammond says come quick, sir! Come now!"

Jack Pryor ordered Charlie Sanders to stay with President Truman and then raced after Ralph back down the passageway.

There in the doorway of a drawing room stood Conductor Hammond. If this squat fiftyish man of bulldog authority had a real first name beyond "Conductor," Pryor had never heard it.

Hammond stepped aside for Pryor to see what there was to see.

Mr. Otto Wheeler lay in his bunk, the sheet and dark blue Super Chief blanket pulled carefully up around his chest, his hands and arms lying comfortably to either side. His face wore a smile, his eyes wide open.

"He's dead," said the conductor. "When Ralph couldn't wake him to get ready to get off in Bethel I took a look, felt for some pulse, there wasn't any." Then, as if to anticipate what the detective might say, he added, "No, I didn't touch anything else, although as sick as he was, he probably put himself out of his own misery. Look at that smile on his face."

Jack Pryor said nothing. He turned back toward the narrow

doorway and saw Harry Truman and A. C. Browne sharing it, both gazing at the dead man. Charlie Sanders stood behind them.

"Sorry, gentlemen, but I must ask that you return to the lounge," said Pryor to Truman and Browne. "Mr. President, it appears we have had a death on this train."

"What kind of death?" asked A. C. Browne.

"A suicide is what it looks like," said the detective. "But I'll keep you informed, gentlemen."

The editor-publisher of the *Strong Pantagraph* and the former president of the United States did as they were told and walked away.

And the Super Chief rolled to a smooth stop.

"We're in Bethel," said the conductor to Pryor. "Five minutes is all we're supposed to have here. We're already running two minutes late . . ."

Jack Pryor reached over to close the window blind. But he stopped. "There's an ambulance . . . no, it's a hearse, it looks like . . . out there and it's moving right up here to the train—to this car. How could that be?"

"Detective, I'd say somebody was expecting a dead body to come off the Super this morning, that's what," said Conductor Hammond.

Back in the lounge, Truman and Browne took seats where they could keep a watch on what was happening out on the Bethel station platform.

"A hearse is already there," said Truman. "Now that's called efficiency. I can't believe the Santa Fe had a hearse standing by just in case somebody died on the Super Chief. I hope to holy hell it wasn't me they were thinking about."

Browne laughed. "I hardly think that, sir. Your good health and heartiness are well known—even to the Santa Fe."

"You Brownes really must be close to the Santa Fe if they'll stop a train in Strong for you."

"Yes, sir. The railroad's always been a part of our lives. Dad used to have a Santa Fe pass and a Fred Harvey pass that meant he and the rest of us in the family could ride and eat free of charge on any Santa Fe train anytime we wanted."

" 'Used to have'?"

"No more. It was a form of bribery—bribery of the press, pure and simple. The railroads had Kansas newspaper editors in their political pockets. Some were Missouri Pacific papers, others Frisco or Union Pacific, Santa Fe and whatever. Dad was a Santa Fe man but he jumped off the train, so to speak, editorialized against it and raised so much hell everyone else stopped it. *Reader's Digest* paid for my ticket on this train, if that's what you're asking. How about you, sir? I would think you former presidents could ride for free on just about any-thing you wanted."

"My ticket was paid for by the political people sponsoring my speech," said Truman. "I don't take bribes either, Browne!"

Even in the weak light Browne could see red in Truman's cheeks, anger in his blue eyes.

"Sometimes you talk like you're writing a goddamn editorial, Browne."

"Sometimes you talk like you *are* an editorial, Mr. President."

"Your dad really didn't cuss?"

"That's right. He believed a man who cusses is a man who—"

"Don't finish the sentence. If I wanted to hear a sermon with my bourbon I'd go to a church, not to the lounge car on the Super Chief."

They fell silent, both watching while the hearse was backed closer to the train and a group of men, including the Santa Fe's Pryor and Sanders, held a conference.

"Our detective friend Pryor appears to have a problem out there," said Browne.

"I think you're right," said Truman. "You'd think a suicide would make it a simple situation."

"I have never, even for a split second, thought about taking my own life. Have you, sir?"

Truman looked truly appalled—stunned at being asked

such an idiotic question. "My god, no! It's not even an option for people like me."

"Former presidents?"

"Nope. People who came from absolutely nothing to being absolutely something. Besides, the Bible says it's a sin."

"What if Dewey had beaten you in forty-eight?" Browne accompanied the question with a smile.

"I might have considered putting a gun to *his* head but never to mine," said Truman. "If a man's failures were reasons for suicide we'd have nothing but women and children left in our country."

"I guess that means you didn't appreciate *Death of a Salesman*?"

Truman growled, "I'd never go to a play about a salesman killing himself. I was a salesman. We're optimists. Optimists don't kill themselves."

"Tell me again, who you are, sir?" Jack Pryor asked.

"Paul Pollack. I am Mr. Wheeler's assistant."

"How did you know to meet this train with a hearse?"

"Mr. Wheeler told me to do so. I do what Mr. Wheeler says."

"Did he tell you he was going to be the deceased?"

Pollack, clearly not used to being talked to in such a direct and confrontational manner, looked away. He had to think about this for a second.

"No, he did not," he said finally.

"But you knew he would be the dead man?"

Pollack glanced down at the ground this time before speaking. "I knew he was very sick and that he was in a lot of pain."

"You knew that he was going to die on the Super Chief sometime between seven o'clock last night when it left Chicago and this morning when it arrived at Bethel?"

"I didn't say that, sir."

"Did Mr. Wheeler have medicine with him—pills of some kind—that would kill him?"

"Not that I know of."

"Would you have known if he had?"

"Who knows what anyone would know?"

Jack Pryor was losing patience. Sternly, he asked, "Let me ask you directly, Mr. Pollack. Did Mr. Wheeler kill himself on the Super Chief?"

"Not that I know of."

"Do you know if he planned to do that?"

"I don't know."

"You don't know if you know or not?"

Pryor motioned to another man, obviously with the hearse crew, to step into the circle. The thin, smiling man in his early forties, named Helfer, did not necessarily resemble the standard appearance for an undertaker. He seemed lively enough to have been a banker—even a Santa Fe assistant general passenger agent, thought Pryor, seeing him next to Charlie Sanders, who had been silently following the detective. They matched.

"Who asked you to show up here and meet this train with this hearse?" Pryor asked him.

"Mr. Pollack did that. He called us."

"What did he say you were to do?"

"Pick up a deceased and prepare him for a funeral and burial—details to follow."

"What name did he give?" Pryor asked.

"Otto Wheeler. I know him. Everybody knows Otto Wheeler. As Mr. Pollack can tell you, Mr. Wheeler was a Super Chief lover—the word was that he won and then lost his true love on a Super Chief ride to Chicago. Probably not so, but everybody believed it and everybody was afraid to ask. Better for the story not to know, what do you think?"

Pollack frowned. Jack Pryor read it as an unambiguous signal for the undertaker to shut up about Mr. Otto Wheeler.

"Is there a next of kin for Mr. Wheeler?" Pryor asked both of the Bethel men.

"No, not really," said Pollack.

"Most of the Wheelers left Bethel years ago and left Otto here pretty much by himself," said Helfer. "Can we take possession of the remains now? Is he in there on the last car—the observation car? Quite a train, this Super Chief. Too rich for my blood."

Jack Pryor was now joined by Conductor Hammond, who

was making a big point of looking at his pocket watch. Jack knew he had a really big decision to make—and he knew it was liable to turn out to be the wrong one no matter what he did. The Santa Fe was a great place to work, but it was full of people who made careers out of making others pay for not following rules.

Pryor knew the railroad's procedures called for removing dead bodies from Santa Fe trains as soon as was "practical and in accordance with the laws of the state in which the death occurred."

"We gotta go, detective," said Conductor Hammond, interrupting Pryor's concentration. "The Super Chief waits for nobody—not even dead suicides."

Yes, a suicide, Pryor thought. That's what it appeared to be. And, by all signs, it most likely occurred near Bethel, but there was no way to know that for sure. Not yet. That brought to mind the Santa Fe's additional backup rule stating the FBI had jurisdiction if the death "appeared to be the result of an action that occurred while the train was involved in interstate commerce." Since the Super Chief was by its very Chicago–Los Angeles operation always involved in interstate commerce it came down to a judgment call—by Jack Pryor.

Pryor simply raised his right hand toward Conductor Hammond. Hold it! was the message. Pryor had the authority to override Hammond or anyone else in such an emergency. He could keep The Train of the Stars right here in Bethel as long as he thought necessary.

Pryor's mind continued to race. Should he at least go back on the train, take a closer look at the compartment where Wheeler lay dead before allowing the Super to leave? But, as all the signs clearly indicated, it was most likely a simple suicide . . .

Pryor told the undertaker to follow the conductor onto the train and do his work of removing the body.

The sheriff here in Bethel—his name was Ratzlaff and Jack Pryor knew him—could sort out exactly how Otto Wheeler took his life.

That was Pryor's decision, which he quietly reported to Charlie Sanders, standing close by.

"Mr. Wheeler obviously made a personal decision to die on the Super Chief," replied Sanders. He successfully fought off an urge to add something smart about how that could be turned into an advertisement for the Super Chief as "the train of choice on which to die."

He and Pryor watched as Helfer and his men came down on the step stool from the observation car carrying a stretcher with the blanket-covered remains of Otto Wheeler.

The engineer sounded the howl of the Super Chief. Pryor looked at his wristwatch. It was still only six ten. Good morning, citizens of Bethel, Kansas!

"All aboard!" yelled Conductor Hammond.

"It could be that Otto didn't use pills to take his own life," said Helfer as he and the others placed the stretcher into the rear of the black Packard hearse.

"What do you mean?" said Pryor.

"There seemed to be a little spot of something liquid soaking through that thick Santa Fe blanket of his, that's what I mean."

"Come on, Pryor!" Conductor Hammond yelled.

The Super Chief was starting to move. Pryor intercepted Charlie Sanders, who had already turned toward reboarding the train. "Stay here," Pryor said forcefully. "Talk to Sheriff Ratzlaff. Make sure the railroad's interests are covered."

"My main assignment was to help President Truman," said Sanders. "Besides, my suitcase is in a locker in the 'Kansas City' car."

"I'll have it put off at Hutchinson and sent back here on the next eastbound."

Jack Pryor took off running, climbing aboard as The Train of the Stars picked up speed to continue its trip west.

Charlie Sanders decided it was all right to fudge a bit about himself. Being a very junior assistant general passenger agent for the Santa Fe simply wasn't going to get him in the middle of affairs for the railroad the way he was certain Jack Pryor would want.

That, at least, was the way Sanders saw it as he chatted with Helfer, the undertaker.

"How long have you been a Santa Fe detective?" Helfer had asked.

"Only awhile," said Sanders, taking a deep breath before committing a lie of confirmation by omission. He could only hope that his tone resembled the way Robert Mitchum—no, Clark Gable!—might have said it.

They were pulling away from the Bethel station platform right behind the hearse, which, like Helfer's matching car, was black and a Packard. Pollack, the late Otto Wheeler's assistant who had arranged all this, was riding in the front seat of the hearse with one of Helfer's men. Another mortician was in Helfer's car with Sanders.

"You must have started when you were in knee pants," said Helfer, but he did so in a pleasant, jokey way. He bought it. Charlie Sanders had just become a railroad cop.

There had been a time, as there had no doubt been for most every little boy who listened to the radio crime shows, when Sanders wanted to be a detective when he grew up. Some of that came from his movies obsession but also from reading the Chicago newspapers, which specialized in gangster and mayhem news.

"Tell me about Mr. Wheeler," said Sanders, asking his first question as a detective.

"Well, the main thing is that we had the funerals for both his parents, two of the biggest and best we've ever done," Helfer said. "Otto's will be a whopper, too, depending on what Mr. Pollack and the family decide."

"Family? What kind of family does Mr. Wheeler have? I thought somebody said he was all alone."

"He is, here in Bethel, which is what was meant. Otto's got a brother and a sister, but both of them went off to Kansas City or New York or someplace and never came back. Otto did go away to school but he came back."

A few minutes later the undertaker and his men eased the blanket-covered body from the hearse. Sanders, like Pryor, had heard what was said about the spot on the blanket but hadn't really seen it.

Now he did see as the stretcher was taken into the huge white frame mansion of Helfer & Sons Funeral Directors. A stain about the size of a softball had come through the blanket.

Sanders tried to deflect his mind by noting that the funeral home bore an amazing resemblance, tall columns and all, to "Tara," the plantation house in *Gone with the Wind*.

"I'm sure you're going to want to get a good look at the body, detective," said Helfer, nodding for him to follow. "I've called the sheriff. He should be here in a minute or so, too. I told him it was most likely a suicide and, because of Otto's sickness, the sheriff understood. Everybody will—except Pastor Funk, of course."

"Pastor Funk?"

"Mr. Wheeler's pastor at church."

Before Sanders had time to follow up, he was ushered into a small room where Otto Wheeler had been laid out on a padded metal table. Helfer and one of his men pulled back the blanket so Charlie Sanders, the railroad detective, could get a good look at the dead body.

Sanders's kid-thoughts about being a detective had never gone quite this far. Before him lay an awful sight—unlike anything he had ever seen, except in the movies. He fought down a surge of vomit in his mouth.

Blood had spread from Otto Wheeler's chest down to the waist of his off-white silk pajamas.

"He blew quite a hole in himself, didn't he?" Helfer asked.

Yes! Yes! Oh, my god, look at that! Wheeler's been shot!

Sanders simply nodded. That was because, among other things, he was unable to open his mouth to speak.

He tried to keep his eyes on Otto Wheeler's face, which was a dark gray-white but appeared otherwise normal. The eyes. They were dark blue. They were staring at something on the ceiling. No, no. They were not staring at anything. His nose. Look at that nose. That is some nose. Round, blunt, but not too obtrusive. And his hair. Blond, good solid blond. Ears are terrific, and what about those eyebrows?

"Let me turn him over for you," said Helfer.

If Sanders could have spoken he would have told Helfer that would not be necessary . . .

Blood was on the back, too.

"Looks like that bullet went right through his heart, that's for sure," said Helfer. "He didn't want to take any chances about lingering . . . you know, before death."

Sanders nodded. There was nothing to attract the eye now except blood.

"Did you find a gun?" Sanders asked. It seemed like a natural question for a detective to ask—particularly one who was desperate for a distraction.

"No, sir," Helfer replied and then added quickly, "I think I hear the sheriff coming in upstairs. I'll go get him and show him down."

Charlie Sanders smiled weakly.

"As they say to the kids at the candy store, don't touch anything," Helfer said as he laughed and left the room.

Charlie Sanders did not laugh.

Then, moving like a flash, he found a restroom down the hall where he proceeded to have his first stress-triggered bout of diarrhea as a detective.

And that caused him to wonder if that movie man Rinehart felt the same about diarrhea movies as he did vomit ones.

Ralph was standing at the closed door of the compartment.

"Nothing's been touched, Mr. Pryor," said Ralph. "Nobody's been in there since they took him away."

"Wait here," the detective said as he stepped inside the compartment, closed the door behind him and was hit with a smell of death—urine, crap, blood. The blanket and the top sheet were gone from the bed. There on the bottom sheet was a thick smear of blood that resembled the insides of a small, smashed cherry pie.

In his twenty-two years with the Santa Fe, Pryor had had several experiences with dead people but most of them, such as the great musician Fats Waller, had calmly died from heart attacks or simply drifted off and away in their sleep. An exception was a drunk baseball player who fell under the wheels of the speeding westbound San Francisco Chief while trying to demonstrate how he could hang halfway out a vestibule door between cars. Jack Pryor had also officiated over what little recognizable remained of several unfortunate hobos whose decision to travel on the outside of Santa Fe passenger and freight trains got them sliced, mangled or crushed. Some, having miscalculated temperatures on speeding trains in cold weather, had frozen to death.

Now Pryor took a deep breath, vowed to breathe in and out of his mouth only, and went over for a closer look at Otto Wheeler's deathbed.

He spotted a tiny round hole in the center of the bloody mess. It didn't take a Sherlock Holmes or J. Edgar Hoover to deduce that this was where a bullet went after it passed through Otto Wheeler. Without touching anything—or even considering doing such a thing—Pryor scanned the area around the bed for a shell casing. There was none.

He inspected the rest of the compartment, first once over lightly and then down on his hands and knees, inch by inch. He found nothing, most importantly no weapon as well as no casing.

Then he lifted the mattress and looked underneath: there

was a spent slug. He grabbed it and rolled it between the fingers of his right hand. It was a .38. Or at least, that's what it looked like. A ballistics expert would eventually determine that for sure.

Oh, yes. A ballistics expert. One in Bethel, Kansas? Or someplace else in Kansas? Where exactly was the Super Chief when Wheeler shot himself?

Shot himself?

Jack Pryor's face was suddenly red hot, his mind racing.

Was there any way in hell, or Kansas or anywhere else Otto Wheeler could have killed himself with a pistol and then pulled up the blanket and disposed of the weapon?

Pryor leapt at the compartment door and yanked it open. "What did you do with Wheeler's gun, Ralph?" he barked.

"Mr. Pryor, I do not know what you're talking about!" Ralph shouted back. "I told you I haven't touched a thing and that is the absolute truth!"

As much as Pryor distrusted Ralph about his Privates business, something about the unexpected force in his denial rang true.

A homicide? Why would anybody sneak into this compartment and shoot to death a man who was on the verge of death anyway from natural causes?

Pryor stuck the bullet slug in his suit coat pocket as another consideration struck him. At this moment there could be an armed killer on The Train of the Stars along with a former president of the United States and Clark Gable.

Hutchinson, Kansas, was the next stop, only twelve minutes away.

The first thing Jack Pryor did at the Hutchinson station was deposit Charlie Sanders's suitcase with one of the baggage agents with instructions to send it back to him at Bethel on the next eastbound train.

Pryor then composed two teletype messages.

The first was to the Bethel stationmaster, asking that Sanders be told to be standing by for a telephone call when the Super arrived in St. Mark, Kansas, thirty-three minutes from now.

The second message was to Captain Wynn Lordsburg, the chief of the Santa Fe railroad police in Chicago. Pryor decided to keep it simple.

A DEAD WHITE MALE FOUND IN WESTBOUND SUPER COMPARTMENT EARLY THIS A.M. AT BETHEL STOP. BODY REMOVED TO FUNERAL HOME. ASSUME LOCAL AUTHORITIES TAKE JURISDICTION. SANDERS OF PASSENGER TRAFFIC DEPARTMENT HANDLING. I REMAIN ON SUPER.

PRYOR.

Conductor Hammond fidgeted behind Jack Pryor at the telegraph desk.

"We've got to go, Pryor. This is the Super Chief."

Jack Pryor was proud of his reputation for calmness, for coolness under fire or agitation. This conductor, who saw himself as a kind of ship captain and the Santa Fe's real royalty, was testing it.

Pryor knew the rules and he knew Hammond knew them, too. Everyone who worked on the Santa Fe knew The Rules.

He said to Hammond, in a harsh, official tone as if reading from the Declaration of Independence:

"I hereby declare this train as being involved in a legal emergency. Under the powers vested in me as a law enforcement officer commissioned by the Santa Fe to uphold the laws of our country, the states through which we pass and the rules of our railroad, I order you to hold this train whenever and for however long as I say to hold it. Do you understand me, conductor? If you have a problem with this, I hereby invite you to get on this teletype or a phone and tell somebody in Chicago, Heaven, the moon or wherever else you conductors believe your orders come from."

Hammond held his ticket punch in one hand, a lantern in the other.

Pryor watched Hammond deal with the temptation to use either one or both on this detective before making a rough military style about-face toward the train.

The detective followed a few seconds later, walking at a much slower pace than the conductor. A point needed to be made and he was making it.

"Did you see anybody go in or out of the compartment next to Wheeler's?" Pryor immediately asked Ralph, who was in the vestibule of the observation car when Pryor got back on board.

"No," said Ralph.

Pryor asked if Wheeler left his.

"No, sir. I brought him his dinner and then came back an hour later, took his tray out and made sure he was set for bed."

Pryor followed Ralph to the observation car passageway.

"This one is occupied, correct?" Pryor asked Ralph, as they stopped in front of the door next to Wheeler's.

Ralph said, "Yes, sir. A man who has been with us from Chicago. His ticket had the name Rockford."

Pryor knocked on the door.

There was no answer.

Pryor knocked again and then put an ear to the door.

"I don't hear anything moving in there. Where was he going?"

"All the way to Los Angeles," said Ralph.

"He really did have a ticket?"

Pryor thought he saw a tinge of red come into Ralph's light brown face but he probably imagined it. "Certainly, he had a ticket. Yes, sir, he had a ticket. Nobody rides the Super in my car without a ticket!"

"You got your master key? Open it up."

"He may be up in the dining car, you know, sir."

"Did you see him go up there?"

"No, sir."

"Open the door, Ralph."

Ralph didn't have to use his key. The door was not locked.

The bunk, pulled down from the wall, was made up with sheets, blanket and a pillow all at the ready. But they were all undisturbed.

There was also no luggage in the rack and no toiletries.

"When was the last time you saw this guy?"

"Last night when I made up the room."

"What did he look like?"

"White as you."

"Thanks. Age?"

"Hard to tell . . ."

"Closer to ten or one hundred? Come on, Ralph!"

"About thirty . . . or so."

"Hair color?"

"Brown. Yes, kind of brown."

"How was it cut? Anything else about his hair?"

"Curly. Yes, sir, now that I remember it was really curly."

"How was he dressed?"

"Neat and tidy clothes—"

"Red, white and blue? What colors were his clothes?"

"Dark blue. Shirt, tie, suit even. Shoes, well . . ."

"What about his shoes?"

"They were black and shined to a fare-thee-well."

Pryor resisted an urge to grab Ralph and maybe shake him. He moved on to the business at hand: "You sure you didn't see him get off the train?"

"I'm sure but, as you know, detective, I can get awfully busy from time to time . . ."

Pryor moved quickly toward the door after having already returned in a flash to his thoughts about this being something other than suicide.

The only somewhat comforting thought had to do with the safety of President Truman. If there was in fact a killer, he obviously came only to take out Wheeler. The preplanned hearse proved that. Thus, it was most unlikely that a crazed man with a gun somewhere was prepared to wipe out Truman, Clark Gable or anyone else besides Wheeler on this particular run of the Super Chief.

A small, uncomfirmed comfort but a comfort at least.

Pryor moved on after Ralph verified that the two passengers traveling in the compartment on the other side of Wheeler's—two movie men—were in the dining car having their usual early breakfast.

A few minutes later, Ralph did his one long/two short knocks.

The door opened and the porter slipped inside.

"A man's been shot to death on the train," Ralph said to Dale

L. Lawrence. "There's a Santa Fe detective named Pryor on board. He may be coming through here before too long looking at everything, including empty bedrooms and compartments."

Lawrence was still fully dressed and looked even worse than he had the night before. "I'll turn myself in."

"You can't do that. Pryor'll arrest me instead for letting you ride without a ticket."

"I won't tell him about that, I promise . . . if you'll help me one more time."

Ralph stared at the awful sight of the man before him.

Lawrence said, "President Truman's on the train now, isn't he?"

Ralph maintained his stare, saying nothing.

"Just tell me where he is on the train and I will say nothing about the ticket."

Ralph, the dealmaker, told Lawrence what he wanted to know and left the compartment.

Jack Pryor returned to the observation car lounge, where President Truman and A. C. Browne were still sitting.

"Mr. President . . . Mr. Browne," Pryor said, nodding to each.

"Am I right in surmising you've got a difficult situation on your hands?" said Truman.

"Yes, sir, I do," Pryor said in as casual a tone as he could manage. "For the record, did either of you see a man come in here after I left you? A man in a dark suit, shirt and tie?"

"Nobody's been here except the two of us, detective," A. C. Browne said. Then he turned toward Truman and added, "But President Truman did hear a sound that could be of interest—even while you were still here."

Pryor took a deep breath.

"That's right," said Truman. "A *pow!* My first reaction was that it was a gunshot. I heard a lot of those in World War One."

"You were an artillery officer during that war, right?" Browne said.

"That's true," said Harry Truman. "I heard gunshots in my sleep for months afterward also, to tell you the truth."

"What time was it, sir?" Pryor asked.

Truman looked over at Browne for some help. "It was before we stopped in Bethel, so I leave it to you, detective. You were here in the car with us, too. Did you hear anything such as that?"

"No, I didn't," said Pryor, "but I was in the back with Sanders, our passenger agent."

"I didn't hear it either," said Browne. "But there was no question at the time that President Truman did."

"Remember, though, that I'm an old man," said Truman. "The Republicans used to accuse me of hearing cheers that weren't there."

"Thank you, Mr. President . . . Mr. Browne," Pryor said. "I

would appreciate the two of you staying out of public view for a while until I can get this figured out a little bit more than I have."

Harry Truman and then A. C. Browne stood up.

Browne asked Pryor, "Who was the dead man—the suicide—if I may ask?"

"A local Bethel man named Wheeler," said Pryor.

"*Otto* Wheeler?"

"Yes, sir. Did you know him?"

"Not personally but I knew of him. He was from a prominent grain elevator family—and a big Randallite."

"The Randallites are no friends of mine," said Truman to Browne. "They're conscientious objector types who really came after me for bombing Hiroshima and Nagasaki."

Browne said he'd heard that.

"Care to join me for breakfast, Browne?" Truman said. "They've already arranged to serve me in that private Turquoise Room above the lower lounge, farther up the train."

"I'd be honored, sir."

Harry Truman looked at his watch.

"See you in about an hour," Browne said.

"I'll be there."

"Mr. President, I'll escort you back to your compartment now," said Pryor.

Pryor did so with a special pleasure because Truman's gunshot report had pinpointed the time of Otto Wheeler's death.

That, in turn, led to the most likely jurisdictional fact that the Super had already crossed the line into Valerie County, Kansas, when the shot was fired.

"I am so honored," said Josephs, a trim man in his forties in a starched white coat similar to those doctors wear. He was beaming. "I cut Mr. Edward G. Robinson's hair on the Texas Chief. Did Errol Flynn's hair—and mustache—twice. Judy Garland's husband also came in for a shave once. But none of that or anything counts compared to you, Mr. Gable."

Clark Gable was seated in the barber's chair in the small barbershop at the end of the middle lounge car. A large white and blue striped cloth was fastened around Gable's neck, covering his front.

"Just a regular shave," he said. "Nothing fancy."

"Oh, yes, sir."

"Don't touch the mustache," Gable added.

"Not even a trim?"

"Don't touch it."

"Mr. Flynn sure did think I did well on his."

"I'm not Mr. Flynn."

"Yes, sir."

Josephs used a brush to cover the rest of Gable's lower face in a white foamy lather that he had mixed in a heavy white china shaving mug that bore the yellow Super Chief drumhead logo.

The emblem also appeared on ashtrays, towels, magazine folders, a variety of paper items and many other places throughout the train.

"There we go," said Josephs. "I hope that feels good."

Gable said nothing.

Josephs, after sharpening a straight razor on a long leather strap, began.

"I've never had a customer bleed to death on me yet, Mr. Gable," said the barber, "if you're thinking I might cut you."

Gable grunted pleasantly.

Josephs continued to shave and make comments, most of which Gable ignored, for the next ten minutes until the job was finished.

The official charge for a shave was two dollars and fifty cents, but Clark Gable gave Josephs a five-dollar bill and told him to keep the change. Gable then honored Josephs's request to autograph the bill.

"This is one five-dollar bill I am never spending," said the barber.

The actor shook Josephs's hand and headed back to his drawing room.

"That was Clark Gable, wasn't it?" said the next customer, who had been waiting out in the passageway. He was an elderly man in a dark blue striped suit and bow tie.

"It sure was," said Josephs, as he began preparing to shave the man in the same chair as Clark Gable.

"What's he like?" asked the customer.

"He's like a king, that's what," said Josephs. "But he wouldn't let me touch his mustache. I would have loved to be able to say for the rest of my life that once I actually trimmed Clark Gable's famous mustache. I did Errol Flynn's twice."

"I heard some lady up in the dining car just now talking about Gable," said the other man. "She was whispering so everyone could hear that he was something close to being impotent. Could that be?"

"We should all be so impotent," said Josephs the barber.

President Truman arrived at the entranceway of his car, with Jack Pryor following right behind him.

A man stepped out in front of the former president, blocking the way. He was thin, disheveled, sickly.

"Mr. President, I must talk to you," said the man, who then put his hand over his mouth to stifle a heavy cough. "It's most important," he finally got out.

Pryor quickly moved past Truman. The detective was a giant compared to this weak little man, who seemed almost as dead as the late Mr. Wheeler.

"Sorry, but the president can't talk now," Pryor said. "Please step aside."

But behind him he heard Truman say, "Do I know you?"

"Yes, sir, I am Dale L. Lawrence. I was an assistant director of the Atomic Energy Commission." He coughed again.

"Good for you. Thank you for your service. You might want to do something about that cough. Where are you headed on this train?"

"Nowhere but to talk to you, sir."

Pryor shifted slightly to one side but remained firmly in place between Truman and Dale Lawrence.

Truman said, "Sorry, but I don't do business on trains. I hope everything's well with you. Have a good day."

Truman thrust his body forward, a signal to Pryor to do whatever it took to make a way for them to continue on through the narrow passageway to Truman's compartment.

"What if we had breakfast together, Mr. President?" Lawrence asked, still blocking the way.

"No, sir, I'm already set. Now, if you'll stand aside I will go about my business. Nice to see you."

Up closer now, Pryor was struck by Lawrence's deathly, unkempt appearance.

The detective put his hands out in front of him and gently grabbed Lawrence by the shoulders. "You heard Mr. Truman, sir, please now stand to one side."

Lawrence had no choice but to give way, but he said, "President Truman, thousands of lives are in your hands. I must speak to you."

Truman stopped. "What are you talking about?"

"Sir, do you remember the discussions before deciding to begin bomb testing in Nevada?" Lawrence said quickly.

"Yes. Yes, of course I do," Truman said.

"Do you remember one on January second, 1947, in the Oval Office? There were several papers and drawings. Do you remember that I was there with other members of a committee chaired by Secretary Stimson?"

Harry Truman looked hard at the man.

"Frankly, no, I don't—not specifically. There were a number of people on the committee."

"Seven. There were seven in all. I was at that meeting."

Truman glanced away impatiently.

"I was there!" shouted Lawrence, an act that caused him to go into a coughing spasm.

Pryor tightened his grip on Lawrence's shoulders.

Truman said, "Calm down, fella. If you say you were there, fine. What's the problem?"

In a whisper, Lawrence said, "I argued against doing that testing. Don't you remember, sir?"

Truman's patience was used up. He took another step as he said, "No, I don't remember that at all."

Truman edged past Lawrence, who continued, "I said the risk of widespread radiation poisoning among the people in the test areas, caused by radioactive clouds and wind changes, was enormous. I said many people could be at risk for various kinds of cancer."

"There were other experts who disagreed. They said there was no danger. Please, now, I must go on to my compartment."

"Those experts were wrong, Mr. President. There are already beginning signs. I am one of them. There will be others—

with names the whole world knows. The testing must be stopped before it is too late . . ." He lost his voice. Whatever ailed Dale L. Lawrence had him by the throat.

Pryor, now behind Truman, gently jostled the former president on and away from Dale Lawrence.

"Think about a remake of *Silver Streak*," Rinehart had said to Gene Mathews as they sat down for breakfast.

"Bad idea," said Mathews, opening *Elmer Gantry*.

The dining car was barely a third full.

Rinehart said, as if discussing the weather, "The kid from the Santa Fe pitched the idea to me last night—you know, in the observation car. God knows, they need to do something to get people back on the trains. The kid pitched Gable and Claudette Colbert to play the leads. I nixed Colbert."

Mathews raised his face from his book long enough to say, "Neither is right for a train picture."

"They were great in *It Happened One Night*."

"That was a bus picture, not a train picture—"

"Won an Oscar in thirty-four, same year as *Silver Streak*. *The Thin Man* was made then, too. Thirty-four was a big year for pictures."

Mathews nodded, put his book on the table and buttered a piece of toast. "They're shooting *Picnic* out here in Kansas somewhere right now—some little towns around Hutchinson, where we just stopped, in fact," he said. "It's probably full of buses *and* trains."

"I don't want to hear about it," Rinehart mumbled.

He scowled and then stared off into the space of Kansas. He had wanted to acquire the movie rights to *Picnic* after seeing the William Inge play in New York. It was a sore spot. Mathews was rubbing it in—to make his own point.

And having made it, Mathews said, "Gable was in *The Hucksters* in forty-seven. A lot of it happened on the Twentieth Century Limited."

Rinehart turned back from the window to Mathews. "Carole Lombard's best movie was *Twentieth Century*, which also happened on a train. That was . . . hey, let me think. Yeah, yeah. It was made in 1934, too. Trains and movies."

"Trains and movies, right," Mathews said. "Eva Marie Saint could be the love interest."

Rinehart, delighted at Mathews's willingness to play, said, "Could we get her?"

"Sure. She won that Oscar for *Waterfront* but hasn't done anything much since."

"Clark Gable and Eva Marie Saint could be great together," Rinehart said.

"Cary Grant would be better," Mathews said. "Must have a good villain, too."

"What about Karloff?"

"Too much Frankenstein. Yul Brynner?"

"Not funny, Gene. Not funny at all. I'll never forgive him

for stealing my Brancusi hairdo." Rinehart ran a hand over his shaved head.

"He had to do it for *The King and I*. But, okay—what about James Mason?"

"British, sinister. Yes, he's perfect. Maybe I could get Hitchcock to direct. He did *Strangers on a Train*. He knows trains."

Mathews shook his head. "Hitchcock does what he wants when he wants and that's it."

Rinehart added, "And he'd want more than Grant, Saint and Mason, anyhow. He'd want mountains. Pikes Peak, maybe. One of those Rockies. Or Mount Rushmore. Yeah, what about Mount Rushmore with all those presidents on the top?"

"The Super Chief doesn't go to Mount Rushmore," Mathews said.

Rinehart laughed. "In the movies the Super Chief goes where we say it goes. You know that, Gene."

"What about the Grand Canyon? It's as big a deal as Mount Rushmore."

"No canyons. I saw too many of those in Utah. Besides, people go to movies to look up, not down. It's as simple as that. Everything is as simple as that, Gene."

And they played out the plot.

Rinehart began. "It opens with the Super Chief speeding across the bridge at the Mississippi—"

"No, no," said Mathews. "It's got to begin at Dearborn Station. Passengers loading, commotion, noise, train horns blaring . . ."

"Mason's a renegade spy who has been trying to steal atomic secrets for a foreign power—maybe the results from those Nevada tests . . ."

"His plan is to kidnap somebody important and hold him ransom for the secrets . . . He's set up an escape on a private plane from an airfield near Rushmore . . ."

"He takes the hostage with him on the Super Chief from Chicago. Grant and Saint are federal agents also on the train . . ."

Mathews: "Gable, not Grant . . ."

Rinehart: "Okay, Gable . . ."

"Once he gets the secrets, Mason plans to toss the hostage off the forehead of George Washington . . ."

"Lincoln's head, not Washington's . . ."

"Nope. Got to be Washington's . . ."

"Okay then. Gable and Saint throw Mason off the top of Lincoln's nose . . ."

"The hostage and the nuclear test secrets are saved . . ."

"Gable and Saint are promoted . . ."

"And married."

Rinehart and Mathews exchanged satisfied smiles and laughs. This was fun—as always.

Then, after a few seconds of silence, Rinehart said, "Thinking back about Utah. Maybe that guy on the train, the one who seemed familiar, worked on *Dark Days*."

"No way," Mathews said. "I knew—we both knew—every one of those people. There were only twenty-eight on the crew, counting everybody, remember."

Rinehart nodded, and he started thinking again.

Jack Pryor had persuaded Mr. Truman to stay in his compartment until Pryor returned to escort him up to the Turquoise Room for breakfast.

Then the detective raced away in search not only of Dale Lawrence, who had disappeared, but also of a curly-haired man named Rockford.

Pryor did the numbers. The "Kansas City" car, where he deposited Truman, was the fifth from the front, almost in the middle, between the dining car and the dome car on this nine-car consist, as the arrangement of cars on any particular passenger train is called.

He headed for the front of the train, knocking on and opening compartment and bedroom doors, asking every passenger, conductor, steward and porter if they had seen either a man in a brown suit he described as "short, seedy, sickly, shifty, crazy" or a six-foot curly-headed man in a dark suit, shirt and tie.

Nobody had seen anybody who matched either description. Which didn't make sense. It was impossible to simply disappear on a train. *Nothing* was making sense!

Pryor ran back to the dining car and went right to the table where Rinehart and Mathews were sitting. The conductor had pointed to them as being in the drawing room complex next to Wheeler's compartment.

"Gentlemen, first, did you hear anything unusual early this morning?" Pryor asked after introducing himself and apologizing for interrupting their breakfast.

Rinehart and Mathews said they had heard nothing out of the ordinary.

Each responded the same when asked if they had seen the man in the compartment on the other side of Wheeler's or, just now, another man, probably running through here, who was "short, sickly."

"Did something happen to that Kansas man Wheeler?" Rinehart asked. "I didn't really know him except to speak occasionally here on the Super. He seemed awfully ill himself."

Pryor, anxious to move on, said, "Yes, something did happen. He passed away this morning."

Rinehart smiled. "Good for him," he said.

Pryor's facial expression must have transmitted concern over that response, if not alarm.

Rinehart quickly added, "If you have to go, what better way than The Chief Way," referring to that well-known Santa Fe motto he had seen on every Santa Fe ticket envelope and advertisement: "Travel Santa Fe, The Chief Way."

Pryor moved on.

But nobody had seen either man. His Dale Lawrence description brought a particularly distasteful response from the dining car steward, reminding Pryor that some of the most discriminating people aboard the Santa Fe's first-class trains were the employees rather than the passengers.

Pryor ended up again at the last car.

He realized that it had been a while since he had seen Ralph, the ever-present sleeping car porter. Where was he? He should be around here somewhere.

And there he came from the next car.

"Where you been, Ralph?" Pryor asked, as calmly as he could manage.

"Oh, I had to see about breakfast for some of my people."

"One of your people is dead, Clark Gable's already eaten and most of the rest of your people, your movie people, are up in the dining car."

"That's where I was, seeing to their comfort. Mr. Rinehart is always one of my biggest tippers. I do special seeing about him."

"That's interesting because I was just in the dining car talking with Mr. Rinehart and I didn't see you, Ralph."

Ralph smiled, shrugged and raised his arms in front of him in an exaggerated way, as if saying only God in Heaven knows the answer to some of our mysteries.

 "How long you been a Santa Fe cop?" asked Hubert Ratzlaff, the husky, bald county sheriff.

"Only awhile," said Charlie Sanders, keeping his big lie alive with his same stupid answer.

"Must have gone right from grade school, I'd say," said the sheriff. "Kansas is one of the few states in the Union that's had mandatory free kindergarten for years. Did you know that?"

"No, sir, I didn't."

"Most of the detectives I've run into have been a lot older than you look, that's all I'm saying."

Sanders elected to remain silent.

The sheriff and Helfer were standing at the table looking at the remains of Otto Wheeler when Sanders had returned from the restroom.

"Helfer here says it was probably suicide," said the sheriff. "Otto Wheeler was definitely a man dying of cancer. Is suicide what the Santa Fe thinks?"

What the Santa Fe thinks?

Here now was a question that Charlie Sanders had never been asked before—about a dead man on a train or anything else. What the Santa Fe thought about anything was what others at the railroad decided.

"All the evidence certainly seems to point that way," said Sanders, giving it as much authority as he could manage.

The sheriff asked for a rundown on what was known about what had happened on the train. It took only a couple of minutes because Sanders didn't know very much. There was very little time between the porter's discovery of Wheeler's body and the arrival in Bethel.

"No weapon then, is that right?"

Sanders told him he hadn't seen one. Jack Pryor remained on the train to handle that part of the investigation.

"I know Jack Pryor," said the sheriff. "He's been around awhile. Knows his stuff except when he thinks the Santa Fe Railroad has more authority than the people of Valerie County, Kansas, as he's been known to do."

Charlie Sanders chose, on behalf of the Santa Fe, not to speak to that issue.

"Do you know about the connection between Valerie County and the Santa Fe?" asked the sheriff.

Sanders shook his head.

"Valerie was the wife of a Santa Fe vice president when they founded our town, so they named us after her," said the sheriff. Then back to business, he asked, "Do you know where the Super Chief actually was when the shot was fired—when Otto Wheeler shot himself?"

Again, Sanders said that, presumably, was also under investigation.

"How sure are you that it happened in my county?"

"Not sure at all, sir."

"In the State of Kansas?"

"Pryor's the one who's working on that, sir."

"I hope to Randallite hell the FBI doesn't get involved in this," said the sheriff.

Randallite hell? Sanders could only assume it was worse than the regular hell.

When neither Sanders nor Helfer responded, Sheriff Ratzlaff added, "Most FBI agents are lawyers, the others are accountants and they're all afraid to say or do anything that might get them transferred to the end of the earth. I tell them they're already in Kansas, where else is there to send them, you know what they say?"

Sanders said he didn't know.

"Butte. Butte, Montana. That's the place nobody in the FBI wants to go."

Sanders had never been to Butte, Montana, because it was not served by the Santa Fe. He knew the Northern Pacific ("Main Street of the Northwest" was the company slogan) ran its best Chicago–Seattle train, the North Coast Limited, through there. It left Chicago at eleven o'clock at night and, while it was a streamliner with sleeping cars and a decent dining car, it wasn't even close to being in the class of the Super Chief. Besides movies, the other interest Sanders had pursued as a kid was trains. Garrison, Indiana, was served by four major railroads on the way east from Chicago, as well as what was called the South Shore Line, an electric commuter service.

"Anybody talked to the church folks yet?" the sheriff asked Helfer.

"Not that I know of."

"The cause of death isn't going to please Pastor Funk now, is it?"

"Maybe because it's a Wheeler he'll make an exception."

"Not likely at all and you know it, don't you?" the sheriff

said. "You ever had him make an exception for one of your customers?"

Helfer didn't answer.

To Sanders, Helfer said, "My boys are now going to take off Mr. Wheeler's clothes so everybody can see what was done by the bullet. Do you want the clothes as evidence or something?"

"I'll take them when you're finished," said the sheriff. "We have a death here that is at least temporarily under our jurisdiction until somebody comes along and tells me differently. Is the Santa Fe all right with that, detective?"

Sanders, on behalf of the Santa Fe, said he was all right with that. "I think," he added.

"You are welcome to stay and observe now," Helfer said to Sanders.

Again, speaking on behalf of the Santa Fe, Sanders said he'd take a pass on the opportunity to see Mr. Wheeler's bloody body completely naked. He had already seen enough, thank you.

He walked out of the room with the sheriff.

"I don't understand the church issue you were talking about just now," Sanders said once they were in the hallway.

"Otto Wheeler was big, big in the most conservative wing of the Randallite Church—that's what most of us are around here, Randallites—which doesn't approve of suicide. It's a sin. You can't be blessed and sent off to Heaven unless you've confessed all your sins, and how can you confess you killed yourself after you're dead? Most of the pastors around here don't make a big deal about it, though, and go ahead to do the full funeral with all the church trimmings. But not Pastor Funk. He's old and old-fashioned, he's rigid, he's stubborn. He won't say so much as a prayer over you if you take it upon yourself to end your life."

"So that would mean what exactly for Mr. Wheeler?"

"No funeral in the church or burial in the church cemetery, for sure. Maybe no preacher presiding even if the service is held in a hotel coffee shop or the waiting room at the train station. We Randallites aren't prone to suicide but the few that have popped up who weren't even members of Funk's church got nothing because he pressured other pastors to toe his line, too."

At that moment, a plump fortyish woman came down the stairs. Sanders remembered seeing her sitting behind a desk when they came in.

"You're the Santa Fe man?" she said.

Charlie Sanders said he was indeed. *I am the Santa Fe man!*

"They want you back at the train station by 6:47 to take a call from a Detective Pryor in St. Mark," said the woman.

"The Super doesn't stop at St. Mark," Sanders said, mostly to himself.

Conductor Hammond, after protesting, bowed to Pryor's authority and a little bit of Santa Fe history was made. For the first time ever the Super Chief came to a full rest in St. Mark, Kansas, population 1,735. Until now, only local trains stopped here.

Pryor flashed his gold pointed-star Special Agent badge to a startled station agent and headed for the first office with a telephone and a door that could be closed for privacy.

"Tell me it was suicide, as we thought, and not murder," Pryor said to Charlie Sanders almost immediately once the connection was made.

"I certainly hope it was murder," Sanders said. "That would be great."

"Great? What in the hell are you talking about, Sanders? Murder on a Santa Fe train is never great! Are you crazy? Drunk?"

Pryor was the one who was on the verge of going crazy. He yelled silently at himself and at the heavens for not having stayed in Bethel himself after that spot turned up on the blanket, for having let some kid passenger traffic agent office boy "handle" the Wheeler death.

"I mean only that it's great that Mr. Wheeler can have a real church funeral if it's ruled murder instead of suicide," Sanders said.

And then he quickly explained to Pryor what the Randallites believe about suicide and how a particular Randallite preacher was likely to punish the late Mr. Wheeler.

Pryor listened, understood but then yelled: "So what was it? Murder or suicide?"

"The sheriff's still working on that 'or' part," Sanders said.

Pryor quickly told Sanders what *he* knew—and didn't know—about what happened on the Super that pointed toward murder, whatever the Randallites might want. No weapon, no shell casings were found. There was a man in the compartment next to Wheeler's. He'd disappeared from the train. His bunk wasn't even slept in.

"Maybe he slipped off the train there in Bethel during the commotion," Pryor said. "Tell the sheriff all this and go with him to the station and ask everyone who was around this morning when the Super Chief was in the station if they saw this man get off the train. He was a white man, dark curly hair, suit, shirt and tie. He was traveling under the name Rockford. That's all I know. Are you on it, Sanders?"

"I'm on it," said Charlie Sanders, who would have sworn Pryor had habitually called him by his first name before now— before their business turned so serious.

Jack Pryor had one last and most important question for the kid passenger traffic agent office boy.

"Is Sheriff Ratzlaff officially taking jurisdiction over the Wheeler case, whatever kind it may turn out to be?"

"Yes," Sanders said. "Well, at least temporarily."

"Tell him the time of death has been determined by a most credible witness," Pryor said. "He heard a gunshot at a particular time when we know the Super had already crossed into Valerie County."

"I'll tell the sheriff," Sanders said.

"Tell him the witness was Harry S Truman," Pryor said.

Still in the dining car, Rinehart said to Mathews, "So, how about *Gantry*? Is there a picture there?"

"Yeah. Maybe we could get Gable to play the preacher," said Mathews with a laugh.

"No way Clark works in a preacher picture," Rinehart said. "That would be like Widmark doing a comedy."

Mathews grinned, shrugged.

Rinehart said, "I don't have to tell you that Clark's got that bastard daughter with Loretta Young he won't acknowledge or support. The kid—a girl in her teens now—doesn't even know. Everybody else in Hollywood knows but her."

Mathews wasn't listening. He already knew all that was known about Clark Gable. He was one of the Everybodies. But Rinehart finished the indictment anyway.

"He shaves all the hair off his body. Everywhere except over his lip where that mustache is. Not just the head like Yul Brynner and I do. But off his chest, his arms—I mean everywhere. Takes four or five showers a day. He's a clean freak, not in a league with Howard Hughes but close. He's got false teeth. The women call him Bad Breath behind his back."

"Jesus, Dar, give it a break," Mathews said, looking up from his book. "Everybody knows all that."

"And those ears. They're as large and floppy as lily pads. He wears his hair long on the sides to hide it—"

"I know, I know," Mathews interrupted to finish the point. "They taped his ears to the sides of his head they looked so bad. They were calling him Donald Duck behind his back. That kid of his and Loretta Young's has his ears. It was so bad Loretta had 'em fixed by surgery when she was six or seven. She was afraid the kid looked too much like Clark. That's it. Now let me get back to reading."

Rinehart looked out the window at the passing early morning landscape of western Kansas. "He's a coward, too. The reason he's on this train isn't because he loves the Super so much. The big American hero hasn't been on an airplane since Carole Lombard went down in that airliner crash in forty-two. Think about that."

Mathews shut the book again and pushed it aside. "Enough of this," he said. "Clark Gable enlisted in the Army Air Force after Carole died even though he was too old to be drafted and he didn't have to. He trained and flew as a tail gunner on a B-17, took movies on raids, won some medals. He may be a whiskey-soaked hairless whoremonger with smelly false teeth and floppy ears but he's no coward, Dar. Just because he won't speak to you doesn't rate all this."

Darwin Rinehart resumed looking out at Kansas.

And after a while he said to Mathews, "I'm back to thinking that guy on the train—the ratty-looking one—was a government man."

Charlie Sanders hustled through the Bethel train station with the sheriff and three deputies in search of a man in a dark suit, tie and shirt.

Sanders had done as he was told. He briefed Sheriff Ratzlaff on the Truman gunshot information and the rest of what Pryor had found—and not found—on the train after Wheeler's body was removed.

And now, in this most impressive of small-town Kansas train stations, they were acting on that information.

The place was classy. The architecture, said a brass plaque at the main doors, was based on Shakespeare's house at a place in England called Stratford-upon-Avon. A red brick structure with white wooden window frames and doors, it was four stories high and almost a city block long, with at least twenty long rows of polished pine benches. Large signs on the walls displayed the arrival and departure times of the trains as well as framed advertising posters, most of them for the Santa Fe's Indian-related destinations in Arizona and New Mexico. The floor was covered in small white and light blue tiles; the fluted light fixtures were recessed.

"We're a division point and that's serious business on the Santa Fe," explained Halstead, the chief station agent, a husky man with a large black mustache. He wore a white dress shirt, black tie and a cream-colored jacket cut like a suit coat: standard railroad-issued dress for most male "inside" station employees.

"I don't remember seeing anybody like that get off," said Halstead. "But it was still half dark and there was a lot going on connected to Mr. Wheeler's . . . situation."

Sanders and the sheriff and his men got similar answers from the ticket agents, baggage handlers, porters, cleaning men and all others who were on duty just an hour ago when the Super Chief came through.

Then Charlie Sanders had a detective-like thought. If the man did get off here that meant he now had to get out of town, most likely in the easterly direction from which he had come.

He asked the sheriff to have someone check with the ticket agents at the Continental Trailways bus waiting room, which was also in this building, Santa Fe having at one time owned a bus company that mostly paralleled the railroad from Chicago to the West.

Then Sanders began studying the big train schedule board under Departures. No eastbound trains had stopped here since the Super Chief. The next one was The Chicagoan, a combination sleeper-chair streamliner due from Wichita, Oklahoma City, Dallas and points south at 8:40, just half an hour from now.

This would be the killer's first opportunity to get out of town on a train.

Sanders scanned the waiting room once again and, to his surprise, saw a familiar face enter through the main doors leading in from the street. It took a second or two for him to place the man as the assistant to the late Mr. Wheeler. Pollack, wasn't that his name? Sanders hadn't seen him after they arrived at the funeral home with Wheeler's body.

"You leaving town, sir?" Sanders asked Pollack, who had not seen him approaching. Pollack lurched back as if he'd been whacked with a two-by-four.

"No, no," he said.

"On behalf of the Santa Fe, let me say that we stand ready to assist you in any way we can," said Sanders.

"Thank you," said Pollack, who steadied himself and even seemed to brighten a bit. "I'm shocked that someone would murder him . . . but at least, well . . . his suffering has ended."

Murder him. Those words jarred Charlie Sanders. They were said so directly, almost casually.

Sheriff Ratzlaff joined them and exchanged greetings with Pollack, who then said, "I just came by to see if a friend . . . an old childhood friend of Mr. Wheeler's was here. I had heard he might leave town and might not yet know about Mr. Wheeler's passing. But I don't see him around the station. So I must have gotten wrong information."

And he turned and left the waiting room—almost at a running pace.

The sheriff said to Sanders, "My deputy says there have been two buses out of here since the Super Chief. Nobody got on who fit our white man/dark clothes description."

Sanders made his case to the sheriff about the Chicagoan possibility and, thirty minutes later, on time, the Chicagoan arrived.

One of the deputies was checking on the platform near the end of the ten-car train, another up front behind the engine while Sanders, the sheriff and a third deputy took up watch on the middle cars.

In the few minutes the train was in the station, less than a dozen passengers boarded. None of them was a white man in dark clothes.

"The next train is at eleven o'clock," said Sanders. "It's a slowboat LA–Kansas City local—Train #4. Maybe our man is waiting for it. Maybe he figured the Chicagoan would be watched."

"Yeah, and maybe you're the Lone Ranger and I'm Tonto," said Sheriff Ratzlaff. "Tonto say, You do what you think you need to do, Lone Ranger. I'm going to get some breakfast and then head to the office and see what else needs to be done in my county today besides hang out at this train station looking for a man who may have killed Otto Wheeler on the Super Chief who nobody saw get off the train but he may have and may now be waiting for an opportunity to sneak onto another train back to Chicago or wherever."

Charlie Sanders understood the message. "Thanks for coming over here with me, sheriff. We appreciate what you're doing by taking official jurisdiction over Mr. Wheeler's death, too."

Sanders had thanked him before, but he felt it ought to be said again—on behalf of Jack Pryor and the Santa Fe.

"Want to join us for a Randallite breakfast?" the sheriff asked.

Sanders declined. He didn't know what he was going to do—*should* do—but having a Randallite breakfast, whatever it was, didn't seem right.

"I have to ask, sheriff," he said. "What exactly is a Randallite breakfast?"

"Crisp bacon, runny scrambled eggs, buttermilk biscuits, apple juice mixed with orange juice, coffee with cream and sugar and a thirty-second saying of grace with your eyes closed and your utensils at the ready."

Sanders's face must have said, I don't get it, loud and clear.

"A Randallite's breakfast is just like everybody else's," said the sheriff. "That's the message. So is most everything else about us—but not quite *every* everything." He gave Sanders an all-in-fun pat on the shoulder and left with his crew.

Sanders stood there by himself in the middle of the waiting room for a few seconds. Now what? was the question for the moment. The only answer that came to him was why not have a look around Bethel for that white man in the dark clothes?

Then he remembered his suitcase, which he had not had time to retrieve from the Super Chief. It was a small leather case his mother had given him when he went off to college; it didn't have much in it besides a change of underwear, a couple of shirts and ties and his shaving kit. But it would be nice to have. Maybe Jack Pryor had, in fact, remembered to put it off at Hutchinson and it came to Bethel just now on the Chicagoan.

He walked outside on the platform to the main baggage room and there on an unloaded cart was his case. *Thank you, Jack.*

But he stopped abruptly and turned back toward the waiting room, then kept on going through the main door and outside to the street.

A walk around Bethel, Kansas, to see whatever there was to see, struck him as a particularly good detective thing to do—*now.*

Truman and Browne had barely noticed the brief stop at St. Mark. They were working on their second cup of coffee in the Turquoise Room, advertised by the Santa Fe as the only private dining room on any train in America. A small room that seated twelve or so at various-sized tables that could be arranged to suit the crowd, it had turquoise-colored decor related to various birds and other Navajo signs and symbols. It was available to Super Chief passengers by reservation only, for intimate dinners and cocktail parties as well as special occasions such as breakfast served by an attentive waiter for a former president of the United States.

Jack Pryor, having delivered his prized possession, Harry Truman, to breakfast with a promise to return shortly, was gone in further search for both the sickly man and the man in dark.

And then, from out of a small Turquoise Room closet in which only a tiny man could have hidden, Dale Lawrence emerged, shabby and coughing as ever.

"Mr. President," he said. "Please, sir. Hear me out. That's all I ask."

The attentive waiter had gone to fetch orange juice and a plate of small sweet rolls. A. C. Browne, sitting across from Truman, grabbed the table knife by his right hand.

Harry Truman made no movement or any sign of alarm. "All right, all right," he said to Lawrence. "Sit down, say your piece and then leave Browne and me alone so we can have our breakfast."

Lawrence, moving slowly as if in pain, grabbed a chair and drew it up to the table between Truman and Browne, who took his hand off the knife. Truman had not told Browne about the earlier incident with Lawrence, so he didn't know what was going on—or why.

Lawrence opened his mouth to speak, but before he could he threw his right hand up to his mouth to muffle a cough.

Truman and Browne, almost as one on instinct, threw white linen napkins up over their own mouths and noses.

Truman said, "You need to see a doctor, not me. I don't have the time or the inclination to argue with you or with anybody else about the atomic bomb, testing or anything else like it."

Lawrence said, "What about those people downwind from the Nevada testing grounds?"

"What about 'em?"

"You and I are killing them, Mr. President."

Browne picked up the knife again.

"History's going to be awful to you, Harry S Truman," Lawrence said, now able to speak barely above a whisper.

"Pleasing history was not my job as president. It was to end that awful war, save the lives of American people, build more bombs for the future, test them and move toward converting our nuclear program to peaceful power."

"You unleashed the most horrific killing machine in history."

"That's right and I'm proud of it. End of discussion."

Dale Lawrence, who seemed even smaller and weaker now than he did a few minutes ago, said, "I'm not talking just about the bombs that hit Japan, Mr. President. I'm talking about 'Dirty Harry' and many more like it."

" 'Dirty Harry'?" Browne asked, speaking his first words since this exchange began.

Lawrence, looking only at Truman, said, "It was a thirty-two-kiloton device that was exploded on May 19, 1953, in Yucca Flat, Nevada. Another right before was fifty-one kilotons, four times the power of the Hiroshima explosion."

"I was gone by 1953."

"I have tried to talk to President Eisenhower. Nobody around him will even give me an audience. You made the decision to do the tests. There were eleven alone in 1953, at least forty since. I was there for all of them. The wind has blown radioactive clouds as far away as two thousand miles. I've done the testing myself. Who knows how many people are at risk, maybe even some famous people."

Truman, no longer trying to drink his coffee, said, "Risk from what, exactly? I remember our briefings. They said the radiation would dissipate with no harm left for any living thing."

"That is not what is happening, Mr. President."

"Well, that's what you say. I'm no longer involved, I have no information, no power to do anything even if I did."

"You're the man who started the whole thing, Mr. President. You are responsible."

Truman's face showed anger. But all he did was shake his head. "I don't accept that, Mr.— What did you say your name was? I'm sorry."

"Lawrence. Dale L. Lawrence. The *L* is for Landrum."

"I will stand by the record, by history," Truman said, holding back profanities he most likely had in mind to speak. "Now, sir, Browne and I would like to eat our breakfast."

Dale Lawrence broke into sobs.

It was then that Jack Pryor returned, grabbed the little man by the shoulders and roughly removed him from the Turquoise Room.

" 'Dirty Harry' was not named for me, Browne, if that's what you were thinking," Truman said. "Some bureaucrat must have done that test naming through an alphabetical system— like storms."

A. C. Browne's only response was a smile.

The air was as fresh as a field of wheat sprouting up out of the fertile Kansas soil after a long winter . . .

O beautiful, for spacious skies,
For amber waves of grain,
For purple mountain majesties
Above the fruited plain!

Charlie Sanders laughed to himself—about himself. *You jerk!* Here you are, supposedly a detective working on the case of a violent killing on the greatest railroad in the world's greatest streamliner, and your head is teeming with songs and company travel enticements.

But in his real life that was what he was supposed to have in his head. That was the job of assistant general passenger agents.

The Farmers and Drovers Bank of Bethel was the first building immediately across the street going north. It was two stories, one-third the size of the Santa Fe station, which, with its many parts and track, was essentially the southern border of downtown Bethel.

Sanders walked over and peered inside the front window of the bank. There were four or five tellers behind cages, assistant managers and loan officers behind desks, customers in lines and at tables.

None of them was a white man in his early thirties with curly dark hair, dressed in a dark suit, shirt and tie.

The main street, which was named Main Street, was almost as wide as Michigan Avenue in Chicago. Sanders knew why. From his reading of Santa Fe material, most particularly a booklet titled *Along the Route,* he knew details about Bethel as he did about all cities and towns served by his railroad.

Cattle drives used to come through here, right up Main Street in Bethel, on the way from Texas to Abilene, Kansas, to what was then the closest pre–Santa Fe railhead to take cattle on to stockyards and slaughterhouses in Kansas City and Chicago. The wide street was a permanent souvenir of those days.

Bethel Dry Goods, the largest store on up the street northward, looked fairly busy with customers. So were Lidiak Rexall, Allison Flowers and a Woolworth's store. Sanders assumed the people were Randallites, who, yes, looked just like everybody else. Most of them, at least. He did see a few so-called simple people, men in flowing beards and wide-brimmed black hats along with women in bonnets and long dresses.

After five blocks, Sanders crossed Main to the entrance to several buildings behind a gate with a decorative sign that said: Kansas Central Randallite College—Founded 1893—First Randallite College in America. Sanders, thinking again of Sheriff Ratzlaff, assumed it was a college just like any other.

Heading back south toward the station and the tracks, he came to what appeared to be the second-largest building in

Bethel, the Olpe Hotel. It was taller than the Santa Fe station but not as long or as wide.

"Coffee Shop" said a lit red neon sign near the hotel entrance.

As he got closer he could see a row of booths lining the large plate glass window next to the sidewalk.

His attention went to two men in the first booth, leaning across the table talking intently.

There he was! There, at least, was a man in his early thirties with curly dark hair, dressed in a dark suit, shirt and tie.

At first, Sanders could see only the back of the head of the other man; he seemed familiar.

It was Pollack, the late Mr. Wheeler's assistant.

Jack Pryor had no trouble manhandling Dale Lawrence down and out of the Turquoise Room into an empty compartment in an adjoining sleeping car. The weak, crying man was incapable of resisting.

"Let me see your ticket," Pryor said once the compartment door was closed behind them.

"I lost it."

"You don't have one, do you?"

Lawrence looked away, saying nothing.

"I didn't think so," said Pryor. "How did you get on and stay on this train?"

Lawrence dropped his head. He coughed once, twice, with his right hand over his mouth.

Pryor felt the Super Chief beginning to slow down again. Dodge City was coming up.

"You paid off one of the sleeping car porters, didn't you?" he said. "He got you on and then helped you stay out of sight, right? Cheap fare, right?"

Lawrence still neither looked up nor spoke.

"Did you also pay him to get you to Mr. Truman?"

Still silence from Lawrence.

"It was Ralph back in the observation car, wasn't it?"

The train's brakes were squealing.

"All right, Mr. Lawrence, here are your choices," said Pryor. "We are coming into Dodge City, where you are getting off this train. I can hand you over to local police and prefer theft-of-services charges on behalf of the Santa Fe against you or I can just let you go."

Lawrence raised his head. "Please don't put me in jail. I just need to rest—to lie down."

"Was it Ralph?"

Lawrence looked away again.

"Say it, please. 'It was Ralph, a sleeping car porter.' "

"I can't do that."

"How much did you pay him?"

"Please, just let me go. Please."

"Where did you get on?"

"Chicago."

"How did you know Mr. Truman was going to be on this train?"

Lawrence did not respond.

The train stopped.

It took less than a minute for Pryor to escort Dale Lawrence to the car's vestibule and down the steps onto the platform at the Dodge City train station.

"I've never been to Dodge City before," said Lawrence, putting his hand to his mouth and coughing again and again.

"You better see a doctor, Mr. Lawrence, fast," said Jack Pryor. "You don't sound or look so good—you're a sick man."

"Isn't this where that famous cemetery is?" asked Lawrence in a weak voice, not waiting for an answer as he walked away.

The Dodge City station was at their window side now. But Harry Truman and A. C. Browne could not see the forced leaving of Dale Lawrence, because Jack Pryor had done the deed up near the front of the train, out of their line of sight.

So what Truman and Browne saw was a long four-story bright red brick building that clearly at one time had been a major Harvey House hotel and restaurant, a saloon and possibly many other things besides a place for the Santa Fe trains and buses to stop.

"What's the name of that cowboy cemetery here?" Truman asked.

"Boot Hill, sir," said Browne. "It's right on the west side of downtown so once the train starts moving again we'll be able to see it."

Truman seemed pleased. "Who was the famous sheriff or gunfighter who hung out here? Wyatt Earp?"

"He was here. So was Bat Masterson."

"What about that Matt Dillon fella?"

"He was made up for television."

"There are always people who come along and want to mess with history, aren't there, Browne. Why can't they leave things alone the way they really happened?"

The train was moving. And in a few moments, they saw Boot Hill Cemetery, which from the window of the Turquoise Room seemed tiny compared to its big reputation. Not more than a dozen or so wooden signs and crosses stood in close proximity at the far west corner of the hill. It took little imagination to see how a couple of trees off to one side might have been used to hang people.

Truman and Browne were well into breakfast, both having ordered bacon and eggs—the former president's were sunny-side up, the prominent journalist's over easy. And there was buttered toast and Danish, juice and coffee. A breakfast fit for both of us, thought Browne.

"I guess you've got an opinion about the bomb and the testing just like everyone else?" Truman suddenly asked.

The Super Chief was back to full speed.

"I never once doubted your decision, Mr. President," said Browne. "You did it to end the war."

"That's right. To save lives."

"Yes, sir."

"One-quarter of a million of our boys and the same or more of theirs would have died if we had had to invade Japan."

"Yes, sir."

"Everybody seems to want to know about that. Here we are ten years later. I guess talk and lies about it will never stop."

"No, sir."

"I know what you want to know," said Truman. "I guess I should have known you came on this train to ask me about that damned bomb."

Browne shook his head. "Sir, I didn't even know you were going to be on the Super Chief—"

"Maybe so but you want to know whether I have any second thoughts about dropping the atomic bomb. I'm right, aren't I?"

Browne said nothing.

"Well, let me say as straight as I can—no, sir. I have no second thoughts, no regrets. I don't care what that Lawrence fella or any of the other crybabies of today say, I made the decision because I wanted the killing to stop."

This man is making a speech—to himself as much as to me, thought Browne. He said, "Yes, sir. As I said, I supported you then and I support you now. I can only thank the good Lord that you were strong enough to make such a difficult decision."

"It wasn't difficult. Only a fool or a nincompoop could have, would have decided otherwise."

"I understand."

Their waiter, a man named Fred, came to clear their plates and refresh their coffee.

"Where were you when you heard the news?" Truman asked Fred.

"What news, sir . . . Mr. President?"

"The A-bomb. The big bomb dropped on Hiroshima."

Fred thought for a count of two or so. Then he said, "I was right here on this train, the Super."

"What did you think when you first heard it?"

"I was happy the war was going to be over."

"See," said Truman to Browne. "That's the way it was for everyone."

"Yes, sir. I agree."

"How did you get the news here on the Super Chief?" Truman asked Fred. "What time of day was it?"

Fred said, "Well, now let me think . . . It was after dark, but the dining car was still open. Somebody, I think it was a conductor, came through and told everyone. Kind of made a public announcement. He'd heard it on the radio."

"What happened in the dining car?"

"There was some hard gulps and talking about what it was and what it meant and then a lot of cheering and then a lot of drinking."

Truman smiled at Browne. "See?"

"Yes, Mr. President."

A. C. Browne began to consider the reality that here now was a much better story than the one he was going to California to work on: how, ten years later, Harry Truman was dealing with his decision to obliterate two Japanese cities.

And what the sick man Lawrence had to say.

"Is there anything to what the man said about the Nevada radioactive fallout?" Browne asked Truman.

"Not that I know of. What famous victims was he talking about?"

"I have no idea, sir," Browne said.

"Makes you think that maybe whatever sickness he has is up here," Truman said, putting a finger to the side of his head.

Mathews and Rinehart had had a great view of Dodge City.

After finally finishing breakfast and their coffees, they had moved to adjoining swivel seats in the glass-enclosed dome atop the lounge car in the middle of the train. They had come here, as always, in anticipation of the spectacular scenery just up ahead in the southeast corner of Colorado and then east to west through the entire State of New Mexico.

Rinehart, the first few times he made this trip, was brought close to tears by the sheer beauty of these deserts and hills. The pastel colors were beige, rust, light green and blue. To Rinehart, it seemed as if somebody with a soft touch had literally come along and painted everything. Not with real paint but with colored chalk.

Now, to Mathews, he said, sweeping his hand out across Dodge City and beyond to the great Southwest of the United States, "There are only so many times you can be wowed by the same thing. That's why nobody ever made a living showing the same picture twice. They're talking about someday putting movies on television—you know, as repeats. Forget that. It'll never happen. You've seen *Gone with the Wind*, you've heard Gable say 'Frankly, lady'—or whatever—'I don't give a damn' and you don't want to hear him say it again. You with me on that, Gene?"

"Always with you, Dar," said Mathews.

"What about *The Super Chief* as a title for our train movie?" Rinehart said suddenly.

"Forget it," Mathews said. "Sounds like an Indian picture."

"What about *The Super*?" Rinehart asked.

Mathews shook his head. "Everybody'd think it was about an apartment house."

"Then, maybe just the one word, *Super*. Can you see it in lights—*Super*, starring Cary Grant, Eva Marie Saint and James Mason?"

"Mason would get second billing to Gable and Saint. But *Super*'s no good. Everybody'd think it was about that guy who flies from building to building in a single bound."

"Grant—not Gable," murmured Darwin Rinehart.

Then, glancing down at the platform in front of the Dodge City train station, he said, "Look, quick, Gene! See him? That's the guy! I know who he is."

Mathews's eyes also went to the disheveled man leaving the train in the company of that Santa Fe detective Pryor.

"He was the Atomic Energy Commission guy who came around before we started shooting there at Snow Canyon," Rinehart said excitedly. "I'm sure of it."

"Right, right," said Mathews. "He had a Geiger counter or something in his hands."

"Didn't he try to convince us that the ground was radioactive?"

"Yeah, but the local people said that was from uranium deposits that were going to make everybody around there rich someday," Mathews said.

"Wonder what happened?" Rinehart asked rhetorically as the Super Chief pulled away from the Dodge City station toward the beautiful scenery.

In less than five minutes, they came out the door of the hotel. The darkly dressed man was at least six feet tall, which made him appear gigantic next to Pollack, who couldn't have been more than five feet six.

Charlie Sanders, from around the corner of the hotel building, carefully watched them look up and down Main and start walking. He followed at a safe distance as they went south on Main back toward the Santa Fe station.

At the corner they crossed Main and stopped in front of the Farmers and Drovers Bank. Sanders stayed back on the other side, pretending to look into a store window.

Pollack went across the street and into the train station while the large man waited in front of the bank.

Within moments, Pollack reappeared and gave a wave to the man to come into the station—and hurry. Sanders read it as a signal that the coast was clear.

Sanders waited until both were well inside the waiting room and out of sight before continuing on. He heard the sound of a departing train. There was that familiar *Whaah!* of a diesel locomotive's horn, and the roar of the big engine.

Right, right. That was the local to LA, Train #4, the companion to the #3 that went nearly an hour later.

Sanders raced through the long waiting room and on out the doors to the platform just in time to see the last car of Train #3 disappear into the west.

Could it be that the man would ride #3 only to a town close by and then board the eastbound #4? Then when he arrived here in Bethel he would simply stay aboard, out of sight of any law enforcement personnel who had returned to the platform to watch the eleven o'clock departure . . .

"Detective."

Charlie Sanders heard the word, spoken by a male voice. But it was not a word he was used to responding to on reflex.

"It's me, Pollack," said the voice.

Sanders turned around.

"I must talk to you, detective," said Pollack.

"Mr. President, excuse me for asking, but have you given any additional thought to what that former AEC man Lawrence said about the risks from the Nevada testing?"

Harry Truman looked away from A. C. Browne and out the window at the Southwest countryside.

"You may be about to end a new friendship," he said after a full minute.

"Sorry, sir, but I ask questions for a living. I can't help myself."

"I used to answer questions because I had to. I don't have to anymore."

A. C. Browne knew he was pushing this—possibly too far. But he couldn't help himself. "I just know, sir, from my own experience that memories can play tricks on people sometimes. And concentration on an event can, in fact, bring back sounds and sights that the person didn't realize were still there." Browne put his right hand to his head to make the point of where "there" was.

He could feel warmth in his face and he assumed it was a bright scarlet, more than bright enough for Harry Truman to see it.

"I think we've talked enough about this, Browne. Just for the record I do not recall a thing the man said. I'm going back to my compartment."

Browne stood. "Thank you. Maybe we could talk again later?"

Truman shrugged but said nothing.

"Clark Gable's on the train," said Browne quickly, trying to reestablish the relationship. "Maybe I'll look him up for an interview. I'm writing something about how television is scaring the movie business."

"Gable's a Republican who came out big for Ike in fifty-two," Truman said. "But, as far as I know, he never said anything bad about me like so many of those other Hollywood types."

"I think he's been so busy bedding down his leading ladies and all the other ladies he could, he didn't have much time for politics. Too, too bad about his wife, Carole Lombard."

"A heartbreaking story, that's right."

"He's also known as a drinker. Would you be interested in having a private whiskey with him early this evening, maybe before Albuquerque—if I could set it up?" asked the editor-publisher of the *Strong Pantagraph*.

"Why not?" replied, the thirty-third president of the United States.

They moved to part.

"We can do it in my drawing room," said Truman. "Gable will probably want it all to be private."

A. C. Browne had to hold back a laugh at the thought of a

former president being concerned for the privacy of the King of Hollywood.

"It's not what it looks like, detective," said Pollack to Charlie Sanders.

Sanders just stared ferociously. He would thus attempt to become the first detective to make an arrest armed only with a scowl. He did have the additional weapon of physical size because he had five inches and at least forty pounds on Pollack.

"Follow me!" he said, also ferociously.

To Sanders's satisfaction and surprise, Pollack began to walk right behind as he marched toward what he knew was a small office next to the baggage room. Conductors and other crew members used it to do paperwork while their train was in the station. Sanders hoped it would be vacant at the moment.

It was. Still in his apprehender mode, Sanders pointed— authoritatively—for Pollack to sit down at a desk that was empty except for a few white Santa Fe memo pads, a couple of pencils and a black telephone.

"Were you involved in the death of your employer?" Sanders asked once they were settled across from each other.

Pollack started to say something but before he did, Sanders added, "Was it murder?"

The former assistant looked away and then turned back and said, "Frankly, sir, I don't know what you'd call it."

Sanders kept his interrogator eyes on Pollack, who continued to talk.

"Mr. Wheeler was told by the doctors in Chicago that he had only a few more weeks to live. He told me that he wanted to die on the Super—the Super Chief. That did not surprise me. I knew why he would want to do that. He asked if I would arrange his death."

Sanders knew he should stop Pollack right now—and not let him say another word. He should confess he was not a legitimate law enforcement officer, not a detective of the Santa Fe or any other company or organization. But Jack Pryor had told him to take care of the railroad's interest. What could be more in the Santa Fe's interest than listening to the confession of a killer—if that's what this, in fact, was going to turn out to be?

So he not only did not interrupt Pollack, he encouraged him to continue, please.

Pollack said, "I thought he wanted me to get some pills or something that he could take after we got on the train. But he didn't want it to be seen as suicide. He wanted a real funeral service and burial and he knew Pastor Funk would not permit that if it was suicide. There may have been other considerations as well—involving the Church."

Pollack's eyes filled with tears. He lowered his head.

"So, what did you do?" asked Sanders.

"I found a man in Chicago who would do the job in such a way that it would look like murder, not suicide."

"And that was the man you just put on Train #3?"

"That's right. He's only going to Sedgwick, the first stop fifteen minutes away, and then he's coming back on the next train and—"

"Keep going through here at eleven o'clock back to Chicago," Sanders interrupted to finish the sentence.

"Yes. I saw that you and the sheriff weren't watching people boarding the westbound trains, only the eastbound."

Sanders took a deep breath, let it out and said, "He's a hired killer, right?"

"I guess you'd call him that . . . yes."

"What's his name?"

"I never asked him."

"How did you find him?"

The water was gone from Pollack's eyes. He looked right at Sanders. "Do I have to tell you?"

"Yes," Sanders lied. There was nobody in the world who had to tell Charlie Sanders anything.

"You're not going to like the answer because it involves somebody who works for the Santa Fe. The only other people Mr. Wheeler and I got to know in Chicago were doctors and people at the hospital. I decided I'd have a better chance with a railroad employee—no offense, of course, detective."

Charlie Sanders, the passenger traffic agent, suddenly wished he hadn't been told anything like this. His job was to know only those things that might help the reputation of his beloved railroad.

So Charlie Sanders, faux railroad detective, simply skipped

the most important question and asked instead, "How much did you pay the hit man?" It was a matter of simple curiosity—and, possibly, a delaying move.

"One thousand five hundred dollars—plus expenses," said Pollack.

"Cash?"

"Every dollar of it."

"Expenses for what exactly?"

"Just cab fare to and from Dearborn Station, a train ticket to and from Bethel, twenty dollars for meals. That was it. His gun and ammunition was part of the deal, what he supplied for the fifteen hundred."

Time to do his duty—finally. "Who was the Santa Fe employee who arranged for the paid killer, Mr. Pollack?"

Pollack looked down, up and away before saying, "He was just helping Mr. Wheeler do what needed to be done. I beg of you, Detective Sanders. Don't make me give you his name."

Charlie Sanders looked at the telephone on the desk right in front of him. All he had to do now was pick up the receiver, dial 0 for an operator. He would—should—first report the entire matter to the sheriff, including the fact that the killer of Otto Wheeler, hired by a Santa Fe employee, was arriving back here at eleven o'clock on Train #4.

Then Charlie Sanders would—should—call the Santa Fe station in La Junta, Colorado, which he knew was the Super Chief's next scheduled stop. A message would be left beforehand for Santa Fe Special Agent Jack Pryor to call him, which

Pryor would do. And Charlie would announce the solution to the death of Mr. Otto Wheeler and that the killer was about to be apprehended.

And then he would report that a Santa Fe employee was involved in hiring the killer . . .

Charlie Sanders's considerations were interrupted by Pollack. "I plead with you, detective, to let this be, to let Mr. Wheeler rest in peace."

"There's been a murder on the Super Chief," Sanders said.

"Yes, but the victim arranged it," Pollack said.

"So it's suicide?"

"No, it was murder."

"Because if it's suicide then Mr. Wheeler doesn't get his big funeral and burial that he wants."

"Yes, and there are other things at stake, too," Pollack said. "Sensitive financial ones that I cannot talk about—yet."

Charlie Sanders's mind was working but doing so silently.

Pollack filled the void. "Do you think it might be helpful for you to know why Mr. Wheeler so much wanted to die on the Super Chief?"

Sanders nodded. Anything to delay his having to make what clearly was the most important decision of his life—so far.

Pollack told him the story.

"Many years ago, way before Mr. Wheeler took sick, he met a woman in the observation car on the Super Chief. It was late, she was traveling alone from Los Angeles to Chicago and on to New York on the Broadway Limited. They had a drink, a conversation and there was what they call chemistry between them. They arranged to meet again on their return trip and over the years they continued to do that many, many times. Their mutual affection turned to love. Then quite unexpectedly and with no explanation, she failed to be on a particular eastbound Super Chief. He never heard from her again but he continued to ride the Super Chief as often as possible, always in hope that she might be on it, too. After he became ill, he did little else but ride the Super Chief back and forth between Bethel and Chicago. We told everyone it was to see doctors but that was not completely true."

"Why didn't he . . . well, make a move to marry her or something before she quit riding?"

"She was already married."

Sanders had no response to that. "So they never saw each other except on the Super Chief?"

Pollack nodded.

Sanders, hanging on to every word, said, "Did he or you ever find out what happened to the woman—why she didn't show up again?"

Pollack shook his head.

"What was her name?"

Pollack smiled. "I don't think you'd really want to know her name."

"Don't tell me she's the wife of the president of the Santa Fe railroad?"

Pollack laughed out loud, something Sanders hadn't been

sure until now the man was capable of doing. "No, no, nothing like that."

"So what's the problem?"

"She was—is—a very famous woman."

"What kind of famous?"

"Movie star famous."

Pollack put his hands before him on the desk and folded them. Sanders had no trouble reading the meaning. This movie story had ended.

"What are you going to do, detective?" Pollack asked.

Charlie Sanders glanced again at the phone, then at a small clock on the wall to his right. It was already 10:40. Train #3, assuming it was on time The Chief Way, would be arriving in Bethel from points west in twenty minutes.

And that meant, first and foremost, he should call now so the sheriff would have enough time to muster his forces for meeting that train and apprehending the nameless hired killer of Otto Wheeler.

But he sat there with his own hands folded tightly on the desk before him.

"Who was the big shot who got on in Kansas City last night?" Darwin Rinehart asked the dome car waiter who brought him a Bloody Mary and Mathews a Coke.

"They're not saying, sir," said Howard, the waiter.

"I'm not asking what they're saying, I'm asking who it is."

Howard, a light-skinned black man in his forties, only smiled. He had won the Bronze Star and a Purple Heart in the army in World War Two. Even though few, if any, passengers knew that, his fellow Super workers did. They had just recently elected him vice president of their union.

Rinehart said, "Can't be one of ours—a movie type. Clark Gable was already aboard. He doesn't rate that anyhow. Maybe it was Greta Garbo. No, no. She'd never be getting on in Kansas City. Nobody gets on a train in Kansas City except that Gene Nelson character in *Oklahoma!* Forget that."

He pushed a ten-dollar bill toward Howard.

"No thanks, sir," said the waiter, who smiled again and moved on.

"I'll bet it's either Babe Ruth or Al Capone—or maybe Count Basie," said Rinehart.

"Both Ruth and Capone are dead," said Mathews.

"When did the Babe die?"

"August sixteenth, 1948."

"Capone?"

"A year earlier—1947. On June twenty-fifth."

"I'm so glad I have you to know everything for me," said Rinehart. "I know Count Basie's still living—right?"

"Yep."

Howard came back down the aisle. Rinehart stopped him. "Can you tell me if it's a bandleader?"

"I can tell you that, yes, sir. It isn't."

"A big-league ballplayer?"

"No, thank the good lord in Heaven," Howard said. "They get all drunked up, start cussing, tear things up, get in fights with each other and everybody else, go after unattended ladies. I dread it every time I see a ballplayer coming. They're also the cheapest tippers, sir, if I may add."

"Are all of them that way?" Rinehart asked.

"All except Mr. Joe DiMaggio. He's a real gentleman, always quiet and polite, always leaves us something big to remember him by. He's as big a man as his batting average. You can't say that about many of 'em."

"That figures about Joltin' Joe," said Mathews, rousing himself to full attention away from his reading. "He's the best there is. You a Yankees fan?"

"No, sir," said the waiter, "the Cubs are my team."

Gene Mathews frowned and returned to his book.

Rinehart took a long sip of his drink and then said to Howard, "You know, there's a Super regular who's worse in another way than ballplayers. Gene and I saw him more than once here on the train. He's an artist who gets on someplace in New Mexico. Paints Indian pueblos, vases and stuff. *Art-teest*, I guess I should call him. Wears a beret. He goes into the dining car at five, precisely when it opens, demands that nobody ever be seated at the table with him, orders the same things every time, including toast that is toasted only on one side and insists that it all be served exactly thirty minutes after he's had a vodka martini on the rocks with a twist. Nobody's allowed to call him by name, talk to him or watch him eat. What's his name, Gene?"

"Rutherford," Mathews said, not looking up.

"Right. Rutherford. One name—first and last."

"I know him from the Super but I've never heard of him," Howard said.

"Nobody has," said Rinehart. "That's the point."

The sheriff's office was in the basement of the Valerie County courthouse, a three-story white stone structure with a clock tower in the center. It was in the middle of a small park a short five-block walk from the station.

Sanders found Sheriff Ratzlaff in his office at his desk hunched over some papers.

The sheriff told the Santa Fe man to have a seat, to take a load off.

"Did you come to tell me that the curly-headed suspect finally turned up and you have arrested him on behalf of the Atchison, Topeka and the Santa Fe?" the sheriff asked.

Charlie Sanders smiled. Whatever he had to take, he would take.

"I just came to review where we were, thinking maybe it was not a straightforward murder," said Sanders, feeling his way toward a most difficult destination. "Maybe it was something else. Maybe it was more complicated than that."

The sheriff leaned back in his dark oak chair, which was a swivel with arms. "What are you saying, detective?" This time the word "detective" came out sounding more like "go ahead, little boy."

Sanders ignored that and pushed on, relying solely on some seat-of-the-pants hope about the judgment of Sheriff Ratzlaff, a man he barely knew.

"Let's say Mr. Wheeler wanted to have it both ways," said Charlie Sanders. "Let's say he wanted to end the pain and suffering from his sickness but he also wanted to make sure he got the full funeral and burial . . ."

The sheriff popped his chair and himself straight up. He was smiling. If this had been a newspaper comic strip a little lightbulb would be in a circle above Sheriff Ratzlaff's head.

The sheriff went into public speech mode.

"Stop right there. It was clearly murder, there was no both ways about it. As you know, I have determined officially that the murder was committed in my county—Valerie County, Kansas. I have possession of the body. I have assumed full authority over the investigation and I have so informed the FBI and everybody else of that. We will continue to search the train station, our streets and byways, our churches and cafés and everything else in our county for the alleged killer as described by witnesses until we believe it is time to close the case, to move on and to let all concerned rest in peace."

Both the sheriff and Sanders stood up.

The sheriff extended his right hand, which Sanders grabbed and shook hard in the manner of a happy constituent who has just heard exactly what he wanted to hear.

As Sanders took a step to leave, the sheriff said, "By the way, I've got a message for you from Jack Pryor."

Charlie Sanders felt the heat rising in his cheeks.

The sheriff said, "He called our office from somewhere a while ago saying you should be at the Bethel station right after eleven so he can call you from La Junta."

"Thanks, I was already planning to do that," said Sanders, struck immediately with the deflating probability that Pryor had told the sheriff that the Santa Fe man on the ground in Bethel was no detective.

And there it came. The sheriff walked out from behind his desk and right up to Charlie Sanders.

"Yeah, Jack told me you were some kind of passenger agent. But don't worry about it. The connection was bad and he was short on time so I didn't say anything about your saying you were a detective. Besides, as we Randallites say here in central Kansas, a man should be known for his deeds not his labels."

Sanders had a hunch the sheriff had just invented a new Randallite saying for the occasion.

"One more thing, for the record just between us," said the sheriff, his voice now down to slightly more than a whisper. "I believe it's safe to assume that there really was more involved in the manner of Otto's death than a funeral service."

Charlie Sanders had nothing to say to that.

So Sheriff Ratzlaff spelled out what Pollack meant by "sensitive financial" matters. "It occurred to me as you were talking a while ago that there were probably some very large bequests as well as insurance policies, written no doubt by our own denominational insurance companies, on Otto's life."

Sanders got it. "And they wouldn't pay off if it was suicide?"

"That's right. Knowing Otto, I'd bet anything the beneficiaries for everything are our Randallite schools, colleges, hospitals and missionaries."

Sanders decided it was definitely time for him to get out of here. He didn't need to know any more.

But the sheriff wasn't quite finished. "I hope your big important railroad doesn't have a policy against murdering one Randallite on the Super Chief for the greater good of other Randallites."

Sanders responded only with a knowing smile and said his farewells to the sheriff.

The sheriff still wasn't done. "I was delighted to hear that Harry Truman was on that train. And that he heard the shot that helped fix the time—and place—of the shooting. Some of our most severe Randallites are peace fanatics who gave Randallite hell to Harry because of the bomb. They're still praying and whimpering over killing a few thousand Japs to save several million of them and us."

Sanders just wanted to go.

The sheriff continued, "But I'm not one of those kind of

Randallites. A lot of us were with Harry on the greater good stuff. The next time you run into Harry on the Santa Fe, you tell him that, okay?"

Charlie Sanders, now at the door, promised he would definitely do that.

Rinehart and Mathews were now back in the dining car for lunch. Both had ordered from the top of the menu, choosing a stuffed zucchini named an Andalouse and the Toasted Hot Mexican Sandwich Santa Fe, each a well-known and treasured Super Chief specialty.

"Get ready, it's almost time—just a few minutes now," Gene Mathews said. And he said it with animation, interest. *Gantry* was not even in sight. "The engineer'll slow down here, if he can spare the time . . ."

Rinehart knew *that*. He was faced toward the rear so all he could actually see were patches of brush in what appeared to be mostly a sandy desert. The great variety of colors from earlier was mostly gone. But he knew what was about to happen . . .

"Okay, get ready," said Mathews. "Now!"

The train slowed, both men began waving, and so did most everyone else in the dining car, including the steward and the waiters.

The greetings were aimed at several people standing at windows in a small-town courthouse. They all had their arms in the air, moving them side to side at the passing Super Chief and the people on it.

And then, just as suddenly, it was over—the faces, the waves and the courthouse were gone and the sand and the bushes returned.

A man at a table across the aisle was on the wrong side of the train and he was clearly not a Super Regular.

"What was that all about? Were they Indians?" he yelled out at Rinehart and Mathews.

"There's a judge in that courthouse who recesses whatever he's doing every afternoon around this time," Mathews answered. "He went away to World War Two from Albuquerque and came back alive on the Super Chief, so he says thanks every day. And, yeah, he's an Indian—a Navajo. Won the Silver Star with the Marines on Guadalcanal."

Gene Mathews looked at Rinehart. There were tears in his friend's eyes.

"Okay, what is it now, Dar?" he asked. "So they're going to take your Brancusi . . . so who needs a sculpture of a boiled egg?"

"I'm going to miss the Super and all of this so much, Gene," Rinehart said.

On the phone with Jack Pryor in La Junta, Charlie Sanders delivered the sheriff's speechy message about Otto Wheeler's death and desires.

"And I have a confession to make to you," Sanders then said to Pryor.

"You shot Wheeler?" Pryor said with only a faint hint of humor. He was a cop who took whatever he could get.

"No, no, not that kind of confession," Sanders said. "It's just that I went along with not telling the sheriff about the guy in—"

"Stop right there!" Pryor barked into the phone. "I know all I need to know," said Pryor, speaking quickly and with force.

"But I'm really not sure I did the right thing for the Santa Fe—"

Pryor finished that sentence of Sanders's, too. "This is over for us and the Santa Fe. I'll telegraph my chief in Chicago to back up the sheriff. I just hope the FBI is willing to leave it alone. Otherwise, they'll be waiting for me in Albuquerque with an army of agents and technicians."

Charlie Sanders made the *second* most important decision of his life—until now. He would not finish his confession.

And after taking a deep breath he said, almost playfully, to Pryor, "How's President Truman doing?"

"Fine," Pryor said eagerly. "He's developed a friendship with Browne, the newspaper guy from Strong, Kansas—every time I see them they're talking, mostly about atomic bombs."

"Who cares about the atomic bomb now?"

"A Private, for one. He came on to harass Mr. Truman for allowing that testing in Nevada. I had to put him off the train in Dodge City."

"How did the guy get on?"

"I'm pretty sure it was that porter Ralph again. If there's money to be made, he makes it. He'd let Hitler on the Super Chief without a ticket if the price was right. I haven't had time yet to make a move on him. I'll do that when we get to LA."

Sanders suddenly wondered if Ralph was the Santa Fe employee who helped Pollack arrange for the killing of Otto Wheeler. If so, that really makes us at Santa Fe a truly unique full-service institution. But he said, "You've had your hands full. What about Clark Gable?"

"Haven't seen hide nor hair of him," said Pryor. "And, as far as I know, neither has anybody else except Ralph and maybe a visitor or two."

"Women, you mean?"

Yes, that's what he meant, said Pryor and added after a two-beat pause, "You've done a great job, Charlie. For a college boy in the passenger agent's office."

"Thank you, Jack," said Sanders.

And now, finally, they were Jack and Charlie.

"I couldn't turn down an invitation from you, Mr. Truman," said Clark Gable.

"Sure you could, you're a king." Truman laughed. "I was only a president."

Truman, A. C. Browne and Gable were seated in the

sitting-room section of Truman's drawing room. Browne had, with the help of Jack Pryor and a conductor, delivered the invitation to Gable, who, according to Pryor, seemed pleased to be asked but reluctant to accept the invitation to join his two fellow passengers. The porter had now served a round of drinks—Truman and Gable both had bourbon on the rocks, Browne his regular gin martini straight up with an olive.

"I admire what you did during the war, Mr. Gable," said Browne.

"It was nothing," said Gable.

"Flying combat missions over Europe is not what I call nothing," said Browne. "You were bombing Germany—or was it Italy and other occupied countries?"

Gable smiled and nodded, as if to confirm it was Italy.

"Didn't you make a documentary-type movie about it?" asked Truman.

Gable again said nothing. It seemed obvious to both Truman and Browne that he didn't want to talk about his war service.

"Your modesty is quite admirable, Mr. Gable," said Browne.

"I agree," said Truman. "Mr. Browne and I are in professions where modest people don't usually do very well. I would have thought that applied to the movie business as well. You're quite a refreshing fellow, not at all what I expected."

Gable smiled and took a large gulp from his glass.

"That outfit you flew with from a base in England," said

Browne. "I read a lot about it—they were B-24s you were fly-ing, right?"

Gable, his glass up to his mouth again, grunted a yes.

"I should have had you come to the White House when I was there," said Truman. "It may not have been that great for you but I'm sure Mrs. Truman and Margaret would have got-ten a thrill out of it."

There was an abrupt silence. A lull. Truman and Browne had been happy so far to do all the talking but now, for a count of three or so, both had run out of something to say.

Gable seemed to pick up on the fact that he had to talk. He said, "I've never been to the White House. That would have been fun."

"Ike would probably invite you if you were really inter-ested," said Browne. "Some of my dad's old Republican friends are still around. Would you like me to check into it?"

Gable shook his head. "No, no."

Then he finished his drink and stood. "I hate to drink and run but I've got an appointment with a friend here on the train shortly and I have some work to do before we get back to LA in the morning."

"A question before you go, Mr. Gable," said Browne. "Have you heard anything about any movie stars' being at risk from some nuclear testing in Nevada?"

"Not a thing," said Gable. He shook hands with his two hosts, awkwardly thanked them for the drink and left.

Several moments of uneasy silence ensued.

"I think maybe we missed out on the famous charm of Mr. Clark Gable," said Truman finally. "What do you think, Browne?"

A. C. Browne looked at his pocket watch and replied, "The man wasn't here five minutes."

"We're clearly not interesting enough for a king," said Truman.

They sat back down and continued on their own drinks, which had barely been touched.

"I was just thinking about something," said Truman. "I'm pretty sure Clark Gable went to the White House when FDR was president. He was there with one of his wives, that actress Carole Lombard, who died in the airliner, for one of FDR's fireside chats. FDR would usually invite an adoring crowd of fifty or so of his closest friends to watch him speak into the radio microphone. I was in the Senate at the time Gable came. A big to-do was made about The King paying a visit to the president. Gable and his wife may even have stayed for dinner with the Roosevelts. I think I remember something about their having a long chat with Eleanor—heaven forbid."

Browne said nothing. He was just thinking about something else Gable had said.

"His aerial gunner and photography flying was over Germany and Belgium—*not* Italy, I remember now for sure," Browne said, adding with a whack to his head, "and I remember for a fact now that they flew B-17s *not* B-24s."

"What are we suggesting here, Browne?" asked Truman.

"I think we may be suggesting, at the very least, that Clark Gable is a man with no charm and a very bad memory about his own life," said Browne. "Maybe all that drinking and womanizing he does has that kind of effect on a man."

"Or could it be, Browne, that the man we had a drink with is some kind of imposter?" answered Truman. "Maybe that was not the real Clark Gable—a pretender to the throne?"

Darwin Rinehart was proceeding through a sleeping car passageway when he came across a man standing in the vestibule between cars. He was smoking a cigarette and facing the window.

Rinehart started to keep walking when he recognized, even from the back, who it was: Clark Gable.

"Hey, King Clark," he said, on reflex.

Gable raised his right hand, the one with the cigarette, but didn't turn around.

"It's Darwin. Rinehart. Darwin Rinehart—again."

Gable repeated the hand gesture but didn't move his head or any other part of his body.

Rinehart raised his own right hand and the middle finger of it and thrust it silently toward Gable's back.

And moved on.

A few seconds later, Gable, having seen everything in the reflection from the window, put out his Kent on the floor with his foot. Then he turned around and raised the middle finger of his right hand off in the direction of the man who said he was Darwin Rinehart.

And moved on.

Still in Truman's compartment with their drinks, Truman asked Browne, "Should we do something about the possibility that this Gable man is not for real?"

Browne had to think about that. "It's probably none of our business, sir. But it might be wise to at least inform that Santa Fe detective on board."

"Right. Our friend Pryor. Is there a law against posing as Clark Gable?"

"If there isn't, there ought to be, Mr. President."

"Where's the do-nothing Congress when we need them?"

They decided to finish their drinks before seeking out Detective Pryor and sounding their False Gable alarm.

"Come to think of it, Browne," said Truman after a few minutes, "how in the hell do I know for sure you're really Albert Roland Browne's son? You talk with a British accent and you wear that eyepiece thing."

Browne took his monocle from a vest pocket, stuck it on his right eye and then leaned over and peered at Truman with the manner royalty would use on a commoner. "I say, old chap, now that you mentioned it, how can I be certain you're not really Thomas Dewey?"

"Because he has a mustache," said Truman. "Just like Gable."

Truman and Browne reported their imposter suspicions to Jack Pryor, and a few minutes later the Santa Fe detective took Ralph with him toward Clark Gable's compartment.

"You sure there's no woman in there with him now?" Pryor asked as they walked.

"Not unless he got her in there himself—all by himself, which is not the usual way. He had a couple last night but said he didn't want any today," said Ralph.

"So how many have there been so far on this trip that you know about?"

"Just those two last night, the first night out from Chicago. Normally he'd be up to five or six by now. I don't know how he does it. He really is some kind of king, that's for sure."

Pryor stopped and faced Ralph.

"You pimp for him, don't you? That is not only a violation of the rules of the Santa Fe, it's against the law—particularly here in New Mexico where we are now."

"I'm no pimp, sir," said Ralph. "The women come to me, I

don't go to them. I'm more of what you'd call a steward, like in the dining car. Instead of showing them a table, I show them Mr. Clark Gable."

"Do the women pay you?"

"No, sir!" Ralph said indignantly. "What I'm doing I'm doing for Mr. Gable, not the women."

Pryor had already had enough problems on this trip without this. But he had to do something about the Gable matter even though he wasn't sure what exactly there was *to* do.

And that's what he was still wondering as he knocked on the door to Gable's compartment.

"Mr. Gable, sir. This is Jack Pryor with the Santa Fe Railroad police. I need to talk to you, sir."

From the other side of the door, he heard a male voice. "Come back later. I'm busy."

"It's an emergency, sir. Please open the door."

Pryor put an ear to the door. He heard movement. Maybe there was a woman in there after all.

In a few seconds, the door opened, but only about a third of the way. Clark Gable was standing there, dressed only in his red silk pajama bottoms. "What's the emergency?" he said.

Pryor stuck his left foot hard against the door to prevent its being closed. He said, "If there's a woman in there with you, sir, I need for you to ask her to get dressed and leave the drawing room." Then, raising his voice, he added, "Do you hear me, ma'am?"

There was no answer.

"What's this all about?" said Clark Gable.

"It's about you, sir," said Pryor, who motioned for Ralph to stay in the passageway.

Gable opened the door and stepped back for Pryor to come in. There was nobody else in the compartment—male or female.

"Are you the real Clark Gable?" Pryor asked, feeling slightly foolish. He had never before this Super trip laid eyes on Gable in person but he, along with most of the rest of the world, certainly knew what he looked like. Browne's and Truman's suspicions aside, this guy was definitely the spitting image of Clark Gable.

"Just look at me," Gable said, throwing his arms out and to each side.

"President Truman and Mr. Browne thought some of the things you said to them didn't add up," Pryor said, the cop sternness in his voice fading.

"I have not been feeling well," Gable said. "I was not in my best form when I was with them. I probably should have declined the invitation but how could I do that to a former president of the United States?"

Pryor apologized for bothering Gable and took a step to leave.

"No problem," said Gable. "Just for the record, do you want me to say it, detective? One of the women did."

"Say what, sir?"

"This: 'Frankly, my dear, I don't give a damn.' "

Jack Pryor thanked Gable and completed his departure.

Back in the passageway, Pryor asked Ralph, "Do *you* believe that's the real Clark Gable in there?"

"Either that or a twin, Mr. Detective Pryor," Ralph replied.

Gene Mathews, looking up from his book and out the bedroom window, was reminded, as always, that the Santa Fe depot in Albuquerque looked more like a Spanish mission than a train station. There were porticoes, small curved windows and covered walkways and even a steeple atop the terminal building that would have done any Catholic church proud. Both it and the attached Alvarado Hotel were made of sand-colored stucco and had red slate roofs.

Spread out on the platform in front of the main entrance were fifteen or twenty people, mostly women and children, dressed up like Indians. They were holding up multicolored blankets, painted pottery, Indian dolls and other such things. The conductor had already announced that the train would stop here for ten minutes and everyone was encouraged to "stretch your legs and your pocketbooks."

Neither he nor Rinehart ever got off anymore. In the early days, they sometimes did.

And there was Clark Gable, smoking a cigarette off to one side behind one of the Indian curios tables.

Gene Mathews, on a mischievous impulse, decided to have some fun with the King of Hollywood.

He grabbed two sheets of Super Chief stationery, quickly filled a page with writing and then exited his bedroom, walked down the passageway, stepped off the train and went over to Gable.

"Mr. Gable, I am so sorry to interrupt your privacy," he said. "I'm Gene Mathews. I work with Dar Rinehart. He's still on the train—taking a nap."

Gable, who was clearly not trying to avoid being seen, said nothing.

"We have an idea for a movie that would be a kind of re-make of your wonderful *The Hucksters*, at least in that it takes place mostly on a train—this train, the Super Chief. You would be the male hero, Eva Marie Saint would be the love interest, James Mason would be the villain. We would get Hitchcock to direct."

Gable took a last draw from the inch that remained of his cigarette, tossed it away and, quickly pulling out his pack of Kents, extracted another one and lit it with a silver Zippo lighter.

Obviously, thought Mathews, The King was as deadly a serious smoker as he was a boozer and womanizer.

But he was no talker. Clark Gable had yet to give any real sign that he was even aware of the man who had come up to him, much less heard a word he said or uttered a response.

"As I'm sure you remember, Mr. Gable, there was a scene in *The Hucksters* that happened right here almost where we're standing. You and Ava Gardner came down from the train, she was holding your right arm. An Indian man held up a suit and said you could have it for ten dollars. You said you didn't need a suit and he said it was for a child . . ."

Mathews saw nothing in Clark Gable's face that signaled even the remotest flash of recognition or interest. Maybe Rinehart was wrong when he told that Santa Fe kid that actors never forget their movie characters, scenes or lines. Whatever, Clark Gable as an Albuquerque curio shopper was definitely no Rod Steiger as a pig farmer.

Mathews was thinking Clark Gable was a bad actor, a real jerk, a king of rudeness, and maybe his breath really was bad, too.

"Great movie idea," said the muted voice of Clark Gable.

"Thank you, thank you, sir."

"Write it down and give it to me," said Gable. "I'll show it to somebody."

"Your agent, your studio?"

"Yes, right. That's what I'll do."

Mathews reached into his pocket and pulled out a sheet of Super Chief stationery. The words *En route* were printed in thin type below the Santa Fe emblem and the words *Super Chief* that covered the top of the page.

He had written in large letters below that:

THE SUPER CHIEF

A major motion picture starring Clark Gable, Eva Marie Saint and James Mason. Directed by Alfred Hithcock. Produced by Darwin Rinehart. Opens at Dearborn Station in Chicago, takes place mostly on the Santa Fe Super Chief. Ends at Mount Rushmore with the death of Mason, who is a renegade spy who has been trying to steal atomic testing secrets. Gable and Saint, both U.S. undercover agents, fall in love, throw Mason off the top of the nose of Abraham Lincoln at Mount Rushmore.

Respectfully submitted,
Gene Mathews on behalf of Darwin Rinehart

Mathews handed the paper to Gable, who, without a glance at what was on it, folded it and stuck it into a pocket. "Thanks," he said. "Nice talking to you."

Then Gene Mathews took out another sheet of stationery. He scribbled a few sentences on it and gave it to Gable. "Could I have your autograph, Mr. Gable? There at the bottom of the page would be great."

"Sure," said Gable. He took the pencil, scrawled a signature and handed back the paper.

"Thank you, sir," said Gene Mathews. "You have made my life."

Clark Gable, suddenly coming to life, smiled broadly and .

walked away. Mathews watched as The King charmed, chatted up and signed his name for other fans from his kingdom.

Mathews figured that he may not have remembered his characters like a movie star but Clark Gable definitely enjoyed the attention that came with being a movie star.

For Gene Mathews, what mattered most was that *he* had walked away with a document that said:

I hereby state that Darwin Rinehart had the idea for me to play in a movie on the Super Chief starring Eva Marie Saint and James Mason that ends on top of Mount Rushmore.

Underneath that was the signature Clark Gable.

Mr. Truman decided to take his chances with the passengers and other members of the public who might be around the Albuquerque station. He needed some exercise, some fresh air.

So did A. C. Browne. And, suddenly, there they were together walking along side by side. Neither said a thing at first except in body language, to welcome the other's company.

Nobody bothered them. Some waved and nodded but they left the thirty-third president of the United States alone to talk to his friend, whoever he was.

A. C. Browne provided him cover—a form of protection.

"How have you occupied your time since we last spoke?" Truman asked.

"Banging away on the typewriter, sir."

"What kind of scary television story are you writing, Browne, if I may ask?"

"It's about how television programs are beginning to affect movie making since the war. I got the idea from Jimmy Stewart. He was a friend of my father's and we've remained in touch. I'm going to stay with him while I'm in California, in fact."

"If you want to know what I think, there aren't enough television sets out in the country to amount to an effect on anything," said Truman, using his walking stick to dismiss the thought. "But maybe one day there will be. You can quote me on that, if it will help your story."

"Speaking of quoting you, Mr. President," said Browne, carefully.

"That was a joke, Browne, for god's sake. I don't know anything about movies or television and don't give a damn about finding out."

"I was thinking about doing another piece instead of the TV one," Browne said. "I was wondering what you would think if I wrote about what we've been talking about, Mr. President . . . not only nuclear testing but the other things as well. A kind of 'Conversation with President Truman on the Super Chief' story. I'm sure *Reader's Digest* or one of the other magazines would jump at it . . ."

Truman stopped abruptly, looked at Browne and then strode off as fast as before.

A. C. Browne had had a sudden flash that Harry S Truman might whack him across the head with his walking stick.

"Permission denied, Browne."

"I certainly wouldn't write it without your permission, that's for sure," Browne said. "But you've known from the beginning, Mr. President, what I do for a living."

"What's the penalty for killing a son of Albert Roland Browne?"

"Same as it is for killing a son of anyone else—unless you do it in Kansas."

"What do you mean?"

"In Kansas it means automatic hanging without a trial. You would be taken directly to the nearest tree, strung up and lynched."

"Where are we now?"

"New Mexico."

"What would happen if I beat you to death here?"

"You would get a trial before they hanged you but only before a jury of Republicans."

"You've got quite a mouth on you, Browne."

"Thank you, Mr. President."

"I didn't mean the way your mouth *looks*."

A. C. Browne laughed, out of nervousness and confusion as much as anything. This was a most interesting man, this

Harry S Truman. How much of what they had just said to each other was simply fun talk? No wonder Truman was successful at politics. Keep them smiling, keep them guessing.

"Speaking of your mouth, Browne, is it just my imagination or has that British accent of yours diminished a bit?"

Browne's smile quickly disappeared. He said, "So that's a No on the story—for sure?"

"That's right."

"What about if I left out everything about Dale Lawrence?"

"Without him there'd be no story, would there?"

The howling *Whaa!* of the Super Chief had sounded more than once. Conductors and porters were yelling "All aboard!"

Truman and Browne stopped to turn back to reboard.

"I wonder what happened to Lawrence? I assume he's still on the train," Browne said, as he and Truman walked.

"A porter told me that our friendly Santa Fe detective put him off the train back at Dodge City," said Truman.

Jack Pryor had spent most of his time during the ten-minute Albuquerque stop talking to an FBI agent.

"Let me guess—you're with the FBI," Pryor had said to a man who was standing off to one side of the steps that led down into the Indian curios store and terminal building.

Pryor knew at a glance that he was an FBI agent. The guy was in his late thirties, trim, average-sized and wearing a dark felt hat with the brim turned slightly down, a dark blue suit, a white straight-collar dress shirt and a solid rust-colored tie. He held a thin leather valise under his left arm, his coat was unbuttoned and a hand was free: to be at the ready to quickly grab a pistol from a hip holster. Recognizable as standard FBI in every respect from fifty yards or beyond.

In response to Pryor's greeting, the agent flinched, then smiled and said, "You must be Pryor of the Santa Fe."

"I am indeed."

"Could I see some ID? It's just routine."

Pryor opened and then handed over the billfold-style leather folder that contained his five-pointed gold Santa Fe Special Agent badge on one side, a card with his photo and official identification on the other.

The FBI man checked the credentials closely and then handed them back. "Would you like to see mine?"

Jack Pryor had to resist a laugh when he said, "I know you're FBI. All I need to know is your name."

But suddenly the FBI man was not looking at Pryor anymore. His eyes were on somebody else on the station platform.

"My god, that's Harry Truman," said the agent.

"That's right," said Jack Pryor as if it were routine. "He's traveling on the Super Chief." Of *course*, he was riding on the Super Chief.

The agent was excited. He said, "Is that Winston Churchill with him?"

Pryor said, as if speaking to a small boy, "No, no. He's just a famous Kansas newspaper editor. His name is Browne."

"Are you on the train to protect Truman?"

"Kind of, yeah. You were about to tell me your name?"

"Lyons—sorry," said the agent. "Rob Lyons. I understand a county in Kansas has assumed jurisdiction over your Super Chief death case."

"That's right. Valerie County, Kansas—Bethel's the county seat. That's where the train was when the body was found and, checking times from a witness, we know that was where the shot was fired."

"My assignment was to meet this train, liaison with you and offer the assistance of the bureau. Do you need anything from us?"

Jack Pryor shook his head and said only, "No, but thanks. I've locked down the compartment. In LA we'll strip sheets and other items from the bed where the victim was found and see if the sheriff in Kansas wants anything sent back to him."

Agent Lyons nodded knowingly, officially. He said, "Until we got the word about the Kansas decision we were prepared to make a move in a big way. Death in interstate commerce, that kind of thing. Maybe seize the entire car where the death occurred and interview passengers and crew."

Pryor had assumed all that, of course. He was amused by the thought of the fit Conductor Hammond would have thrown to all that. Unhook and remove the observation car here in Albuquerque? *You can't do that! This car belongs to the Santa Fe Railroad!* Interview all the passengers and crew? *You can't do that. This is the Super Chief. We have a schedule to keep!*

Agent Lyons extended his right hand to Pryor. "Well, we'll leave it here. Have a good evening."

Pryor thanked him for coming down to the station.

Lyons started to leave but stopped. "Is that Clark Gable?" he asked. "Is Clark Gable on this train, too?"

Jack Pryor whipped around. There was Gable waving to people, shaking hands, signing autographs. Fortunately from Pryor's view, the Gable-doubting President Truman and his Kansas newspaperman friend had walked in the opposite direction down the long platform by then.

"You bet," Pryor said. "If you'd like to meet him, come on, I'll introduce you."

Agent Lyons beamed. "My mother adores this guy. She'll never believe it when I tell her."

"Mr. Gable," said Jack Pryor, stepping in front of Gable. "I have a man here who'd love to meet you. This is Special Agent Lyons of the Federal Bureau of Investigation."

Lyons shook the right hand of The King. "This is a real honor, Mr. Gable," he said.

"I'd better get back on the train—right now," said Gable quickly. "Wouldn't want to be left in Albuquerque."

He turned and almost ran back to the Super Chief.

"I can't believe it," said FBI Agent Lyons. "President Truman and Clark Gable—on the same train."

"All in a day's work on the Santa Fe," said Santa Fe agent Pryor. "If you'd like to switch from the FBI to the Santa Fe, let me know. I'll put in a good word."

Agent Lyons said he'd take a pass.

At 9:45 a.m., an hour and a half behind schedule, the Super Chief eased into Union Station at Los Angeles. The various emergency-related stops and pauses had caused the delay.

But it was still a major occasion. The arrival of the Super Chief always was, with chatter from people, noise from the trains and the baggage carts, the sounds and excitement of return, the pleasure of arrival. Home again for some, California here I am! for others. Chauffeurs and assistants for some, taxi and bus rides for others.

"I was right, the lawyers are waiting for you, Dar," said Gene Mathews. "I can see them. Three guys like vultures, each with a large briefcase. They're all standing just inside the station doorway."

Darwin Rinehart slowed the pace of their walk, signaling their redcap with his cart to do the same. "I don't think I can go through with this, Gene. I can't handle it, Gene. I can't do this, Gene."

"No choice, Dar. You have no choice. You can come back. This is Comeback City. People come back all the time. You'll come back."

"My company. It's mine. My office. I love my office. What about my Brancusi? I love that egg. I bought it in New York . . . you remember, Gene, at the gallery on Fifty-seventh."

"I remember, Dar. It's worth a bundle—that's why they want it now."

"My house. Will they take my house, Gene?"

"Probably. They'll give you the complete bad news in a minute. Look, you knew it was coming. We should never have gone to New York. That was crazy, like I told you. You should have stayed here, Dar."

They were no longer moving. Other passengers had to walk around them on the platform, heading toward the station.

"Look, Dar! Look!"

Rinehart reluctantly followed Mathews's stare. "See this guy coming from the train?"

"Yeah, what? I'm looking," Darwin said.

"There's no mustache and his hair's been combed differently but look at him. He's almost a live replica of King Clark Gable. A little shorter—slightly smaller ears. Wonder what his breath smells like?"

Rinehart said, "What this country does not need are two Clark Gables."

They said their farewell words on the station platform, as redcaps and local California Democrats sorted through the commotion of Truman's arrival.

"This has been the ultimate honor for me, sir," said Albert Carlton Browne.

"I've enjoyed it myself, Browne," said Harry S Truman. "We had quite a bit of excitement on our trip, I'd say."

"A killing, an A-testing protester and, to top it off, a potential Clark Gable imposter—and that's only what I know about," said Browne, then, after a pause, adding, "That railroad detective never said anything further to me about our Clark Gable doubts. Did he to you?"

"No, he didn't," said Truman. "Clearly the detective team of Truman and Browne was not that persuasive."

"All told, this really would make a great 'My Spring of '56 Trip on the Super Chief' story for me to write," Browne said.

Truman lifted his walking stick as if it were a club. "Permission still *not* granted."

As they stepped apart, Harry S Truman halted, grinned and said in a quiet voice, "You're almost back to talking like a Kansan, Browne."

"Thank you, Mr. President—I think," Browne replied.

"I did finally remember something more about that Dale Lawrence," said the former president.

The prominent journalist took a breath.

"Yeah, he may very well have been in the Oval Office with Stimson. I think Stimson may have made me let the guy talk for two minutes—not a second more. I'm pretty sure he made the case for delaying the testing. He wanted more data known and studied before any more explosions were allowed. But the guy was in the minority so I didn't pay much attention. Nobody did. All the Atomic Energy Commission top brass said there was no danger."

A. C. Browne put his monocle back into his right eye. "On the train, that Lawrence certainly seemed awfully sick himself, didn't he?"

Harry S Truman said, "But from what cause? Or what disease?"

"Are you going to look into it further, sir?"

"No, I am not." A half grin came across Truman's face. "And I don't want to read about this in *Reader's Digest* or any other goddamn magazine or even in the *Strong Pantagraph*."

Browne was not grinning. He looked down at the station platform.

"You gave me your word—no story," said the man from Missouri. "I have to go, Browne."

This was not an easy situation for A. C. Browne. He was at this moment a reporter with one helluva story—and he was going to have to give it up.

But he said, "All right, Mr. President."

Darwin Rinehart and Gene Mathews and their redcap stood motionless in a quiet corner of the giant waiting room. The humiliation ceremony was suddenly over, the lawyers had in less than a minute acquired Rinehart's signature and life, including his Brancusi egg. He'd been granted five hours to go to his house and, under court supervision, remove his most personal effects.

Remove them to where exactly?

Mathews suggested a hotel. Not the Ambasssador and certainly not the Beverly Wilshire, Rinehart's most favorite Hollywood place. Something cheaper. They did have some cash, but maybe only fifteen hundred dollars or so.

Rinehart said, "We're getting back on the Super Chief, Gene, where we belong—where we're safe."

Mathews pointed toward the steps from the train platform and the Super Chief. "Look! That's Harry Truman! He's coming right this way."

Rinehart looked. "My God, it sure is. Was he on the Super with us?"

"Must have been the big-name passenger who was in the 'Kansas City' sleeper car," Rinehart said.

Truman and a group of five or six other men passed right by Rinehart and Mathews on the way to the front entrance.

"Mr. President—I was always with you," Rinehart said to him.

"Me, too," said Mathews. "I loved the way you gave 'em hell."

Truman raised his walking stick to his hat to acknowledge the good words. "Thank you, thank you," he said, as he kept walking.

Someone started clapping. And then a few others did, including Rinehart and Mathews. Truman acknowledged it all with smiles and more salutes with his stick.

"There was a lot more happening on the Super than we knew about, Dar," Mathews said, once Harry Truman was gone.

"We'll be on it again tonight. We're going to stay right here in this waiting room until it leaves. We've got enough cash for tickets, a drawing room with an adjoining bedroom. Same as always for us, Gene."

Mathews shook his head slowly, sadly. "All I'll get is a ticket for you, Dar. I won't be going."

"No, no, Gene. Think of it as a story. A failed movie producer goes into a deep dive, flips out . . ." He stopped, waiting for Mathews to pick it up.

"I'm not playing anymore, Dar," said Mathews.

"What?"

"I'm leaving you." Mathews turned and headed in the direction of the station's front door.

"No! Gene, no!"

Mathews did not turn around. He kept walking.

"Think about it, Gene!" Rinehart yelled after him. "He flips out and spends the rest of his life riding back and forth, back and forth, back and forth between LA and Chicago . . ."

Gene Mathews made no sign he'd heard anything as he moved farther away.

If Darwin Rinehart had been a streamliner he would have sounded his howling horn loud enough to shake Mount Rushmore.

Jack Pryor had had a brief exchange of departing words with Ralph, the sleeping car porter. The detective gave instructions about taking the linens and other evidentiary items from the late Otto Wheeler's compartment to the station dispatching office. And he warned Ralph again to get out of the Private business and stay out of it.

"I am certain you let that guy on to bother President Truman," Pryor said. "I promise you with an oath on my badge that I'm going to get you. Every time you take money from a guy like that, think: This could be it. This could be a company plant. This could mean your job and your life. Think that every time."

"Yes, sir," was all Ralph said in response.

Then Pryor went into the station, where there was word in the railroad police office for him to call his boss, Captain Lordsburg, in Chicago. URGENT, was the message.

"Did you put somebody off the Super in Dodge City?" were Lordsburg's first words. No hello greeting, no how did things go with the death of the Bethel regular? *That* was now up to some Kansas sheriff to sort through.

Pryor confirmed that he had indeed tossed a man off at Dodge City.

"He was bothering President Truman, for one thing," said Pryor. "And he was a Private. That porter Ralph put him on board, I'm pretty sure."

"The guy you tossed turned up in Boot Hill."

"The cemetery?"

"You know another Boot Hill in Dodge City?" said the captain. "But he's not dead, not yet. They found him lying by one of the tombstones. He's sick as hell. They've got him in a hospital. Some of the railroad lawyers don't like the idea of a dying man being put off one of our trains in the middle of nowhere—no matter the reason. Did you know he once worked in Washington for the government?"

"I did hear him tell Mr. Truman that. He was coughing but I didn't know he was dying. Dodge isn't really nowhere—"

"Get back there and clean it up. Our railroad doesn't like it when sick people are put off our trains—particularly VIPs."

"I really don't think this guy rates as anybody that important—"

"Just take care of it, Jack. I already got word to that kid from the traffic office—Sanders. He's still in Bethel. I told him to get over to Dodge and cover us in case the guy really dies before you get there."

Before Pryor could respond, Captain Lordsburg said, "Got to run. Some drunk ballplayer's gone nuts on the Texas Chief north of Houston and is using the dining car china as baseballs. He's mad because the Dodgers cut him from their roster—something like that. Talk to you soon, Jack."

Lordsburg hung up as abruptly as he had begun.

Jack Pryor went to the waiting room and looked up at the schedule board. It confirmed what he already knew. The El Capitan, the Santa Fe's eastbound high-level chair-car streamliner, would depart at 1:15, less than three hours from now. And he would be on it.

Pryor turned around to see Albert Carlton Browne standing there, also looking up at the schedule information.

"Where you headed, detective?" Browne asked.

"Back to Kansas," Pryor said.

"Me, too," said Browne.

And a while later, Pryor spotted Darwin Rinehart staring off into space, sitting by himself in a far corner of the waiting room.

"Can I help you, sir?" Pryor asked Rinehart, who just shook his head and looked away. He seemed embarrassed that he had been seen.

Pryor's cop antenna was alerted. He thought he saw something new and alarmingly sad in the face of this man of Hollywood who had disembarked from the Super only a short time ago.

"I'm going back on the Super Chief," Rinehart said to Pryor after several seconds of uncomfortable silence. He spoke in a near whisper.

The Santa Fe detective had learned that often the best way to get people to say something is just to remain silent. He wondered, What in the hell is going on? Two passengers from the Super—the Kansas editor and now the movie man—turning around to head back the other direction the same day they arrived?

"Forget something?" said Pryor to Rinehart, smiling.

"Yeah, you might say that." Rinehart still hadn't spoken in full voice or made eye contact with Pryor.

The Santa Fe man looked up at the schedule board. "The El Capitan leaves at one fifteen . . ."

Darwin Rinehart glared at Jack Pryor. "I only travel on the Super Chief!" he said with indignation.

"That'll mean waiting six more hours," said Pryor.

There was no response from Rinehart, and Jack Pryor finally just walked away.

 It was all over by the time Jack Pryor got to the hospital in Dodge City.

"That guy Lawrence is dead—as of about ten minutes ago," Charlie Sanders reported to Pryor.

Sanders had been waiting for Pryor just inside the hospital's main entrance. He had had to wait six hours in Bethel to ride a slow-moving train named the Grand Canyon, the next westbound, for the two-hour trip to Dodge City.

Now he told Pryor that he had stayed with Lawrence until the end. Sanders said the poor man had been in terrific pain from what the doctors said was cancer in his stomach and lungs; he could speak only in a weak whisper just before he died.

"The Kansas man with the British accent—you know, the one who hung out with President Truman—was in the room with Lawrence the last few minutes," Sanders said.

As they walked up the hospital stairs together, Sanders reported that last night a watchman had come across Lawrence lying on the ground between two graves in the Boot Hill Cemetery. One grave contained a buffalo hunter who had frozen to death in a blizzard, the other a dance hall madam known around town as a soiled dove. Lawrence was shivering, pale, feverish, coughing like hell and talking crazy. An ambulance was called and he was brought here to Trinity Hospital.

Now Pryor went with Sanders into a room where A. C. Browne was seated in a small green metal chair on the other side of Lawrence's now-empty bed. He was writing in a small notebook.

"I knew you were going to Kansas but why did you come

here, Mr. Browne?" said Pryor, unable to hide his wariness about the unexpected presence of Mr. Truman's journalist friend.

Pryor had run into Browne briefly a couple of times on the El Capitan but figured he was on his way home to Strong. Pryor, who'd been preoccupied with railroad business on arriving at Dodge, had not seen Browne disembark from the train.

"I came here for the same reason as you, detective," Browne said now to Pryor. "To visit Dale Lawrence."

Pryor was annoyed with himself for taking his sweet time finishing various reports and doing other tasks at the Dodge City station. Now—too late—he knew he should have rushed immediately to the hospital as Browne obviously had done.

The detective took a breath, held it a few seconds and then asked, "Did you talk to him about . . . you know, my having put him off the Super Chief?"

"No, no," Browne said. "As far as I could tell, his conduct toward President Truman justified what was done."

"He didn't have a ticket either," Pryor said, a bit too loudly, defensively.

Browne resumed writing something in a narrow spiral notebook, about the size of a paperback book.

"So you're not doing a newspaper story about the way he was treated by the Santa Fe?" Pryor asked, trying to remain as nonchalant as possible.

Browne smiled, shook his head and said his interest was in something very different. "Lawrence was able to speak to me only for a few moments but it was all about what he'd been saying to President Truman about nuclear testing."

When Pryor didn't immediately respond, Browne added, "He said a lot of people are dying because of the tests in Nevada." Then, looking down at his notebook, Browne said, " 'I'm one of them.' That was probably the most coherent thing he said. He also mumbled something about John Wayne and Susan Hayward being victims."

"John Wayne's sick?" Pryor asked.

"I don't know," Browne said. "The best I could understand was that it had to do with making a movie in Utah—which I couldn't follow."

"*The Conqueror*, yes, I saw it," said Charlie Sanders, who had accompanied Pryor to the hospital room but so far had remained silent. "It was truly awful. John Wayne was wearing heavy makeup and a drooping black mustache."

Pryor, not interested in a movie review at the moment, motioned for Sanders to follow him and said to Browne, "We'll leave it to you, sir. We're taking the Super Chief back home to Chicago at ten fifteen tonight. You?"

"I'm returning to California on a westbound at eight fifty," said Browne. "I think I'll go back to the story I was working on in the first place—out in Hollywood."

Pryor said nothing because he did not really know what Browne was talking about.

"I wasn't able to get enough from Lawrence to put his tale together," Browne added.

They made their perfunctory farewells.

"No offense, Mr. Browne," said Pryor, "but for a man from Kansas you sound a lot like Winston Churchill."

"There's more to Kansas than an accent, detective," replied A. C. Browne.

On the Super, Pryor and Sanders were met by Conductor Hammond in a vestibule between cars in the middle of the train. Hammond, having napped and freshened up in crew quarters at LA, was on the eastbound return trip. He, too, was going home to Chicago.

Hammond said they were really full of movie people this time—actresses, actors, bit players, directors.

"A couple of really big lady Stars are aboard traveling under other names," Hammond said. "I mean, really big."

Only on the Super Chief, The Train of the Stars, would—could—any conductor talk like this. It made Charlie Sanders proud to be of the Santa Fe family. And he wondered—oh, how he wondered—who those two big lady Stars might be.

Hammond said, "That producer Rinehart is on board, too, if you can believe it."

"Yeah, he told me he was heading right back on the Super," Pryor said. "I didn't ask him why but I figure that kind of thing is known only by people in the movie business—not ours."

Pryor then told Hammond he was most interested at the

moment in finding a place to sleep. The conductor pointed him toward a sleeping car four up the train that had a couple of vacant roomettes.

Charlie Sanders and Pryor said they would meet up later.

Sanders had a question for Conductor Hammond.

"It concerns Mr. Wheeler, the Bethel man who died on the westbound," Sanders said, remaining in the vestibule. "Do you remember his friend here on the Super, a woman from the movies?"

Hammond grinned. "Oh, yeah. She's one of the big Stars. They were a regular sight. She'd get on in LA, sleep late the next morning, go to bed early that evening and then get back up just in time to meet Mr. Wheeler at one thirty in Bethel, first in the lounge and then in one or the other's drawing rooms."

"Then she quit traveling on the Super?" Sanders asked.

Hammond said, "I didn't see her at least and I asked other crews and they didn't either. But Mr. Wheeler kept riding, even after he got so sick. There was a routine chore for his porter—usually Ralph—to check out the train from one end to the other for his girlfriend."

Sanders took a deep breath. "Who is she?"

Hammond looked at Charlie Sanders, then down at his leather pouch where he carried tickets and other papers, then out the window of the moving train.

"I don't think I should tell you that, Mr. Sanders," said Hammond. "I'm thinking Jack Pryor's got it right about what's anybody's business—including the Santa Fe's."

"Everybody knows about Clark Gable and his goings-on," said Sanders, still a little full of himself from his successful debut as a faux detective. "Movie star business is everybody's business. I don't get the secrecy about Mr. Wheeler and his friend."

The conductor replied as if issuing a papal edict, "This is different. Now he's dead. She's married. It wouldn't be fair."

"Half the women Gable's gone to bed with on this train and elsewhere were married, too, I'll bet." Sanders had to control himself. He was aware his voice was rising, something this little exchange truly did not rate.

"That's his reputation and he lives up to it," said Hammond. "This woman's reputation is for other things. It's not for me to smear it. Sorry. But if you find her on your own, so be it. That's your business, not mine."

"Find her? You mean she's one of the two you were talking about on *this* train?" Charlie Sanders said, almost shouting.

Hammond shrugged and started to leave. "Why do you want to talk to her anyhow? I hope you're not just being nosy."

Sanders had to think about that a couple of seconds. "I think she should know about Otto Wheeler's death." He knew it was a weak point the minute he said it.

Hammond, moving away, said, "I've got to walk the train and start getting ready for Bethel and Kansas City."

So be it, indeed, thought Sanders. It really was none of his business. Okay, maybe it was . . . a little. There might be a role for a beautiful woman in the Super Chief movie.

He decided he would head to the observation car lounge, where he would just sit for a while. There were empty roomettes that he could, like Jack Pryor, use but suddenly he was too excited to sleep.

Who are those two big lady movie stars?

Sanders passed through three cars to the deserted lounge at the end of the train.

He found a place behind the magazine rack for his suitcase, stuck it there and looked through the darkness at the rest of the car. He switched on one of the tiny wall lamps and decided he would take one of the two chairs on either side of the rear window at the very end of the car.

He was no sooner seated when he heard noise from the door opening at the far end of the car. Then a shadow appeared at the doorway into the lounge. It was a woman—a small woman.

Charlie Sanders stood.

"Good evening, ma'am," he said.

The woman stopped. "I'm sorry," she said. "I didn't expect anyone to be in here this time of night."

Charlie Sanders recognized the voice—or, at least, he thought he did. It was deep for a woman's, foreign sounding.

"I'm Charlie Sanders of the Santa Fe—I'm an assistant general passenger agent," he said. "I'm on board to assist passengers in any way I can."

That caused the woman to continue her walk toward him. "Nice to meet you, Mr. Sanders."

In passing lights and the side lamp he could see that the woman was carrying an open book. No, it was larger than a book. It seemed like papers stapled together in a folder. Her skirt was long, inches below the knee, and her hair was cut short.

Then he saw her face. Oh, my god! "Claudette Colbert! You're Claudette Colbert!"

"I am indeed," she said, arriving in front of him. "Thank you for noticing." Her voice was as sophisticated and quiet and appealing as it sounded in the movies. Her vowels. They were so round and full.

Claudette Colbert! This is Claudette Colbert!

She closed the folder and put it under her left arm, extending her right hand toward him.

He took her hand into his own and then didn't know what to do with it. Shake it? Hold it for the count of five? Hold it with both of his for a count of five—or ten?

She put him out of his misery by removing it herself. Then she patted the folder against her left hip and said, "This is a script for a play I'm going to do in New York. It's a comeback of sorts on the stage. I decided to go on the train so I could lock myself away, get into the part. One of my first roles was in a Broadway play called *The Ghost Train*. A bunch of weird characters get stranded at a small-town train station in Britain. It was in 1926, played only sixty-one performances . . . but you don't want to know about all that at two in the morning."

You talk so beautifully in person!

"Oh, Miss Colbert, I am just so thrilled to meet you. You can say anything you wish for as long as you wish. You are one of my most favorite of the favorites."

"Thank you," she said sweetly but with what Sanders read as a signal that she had no intention of saying much of anything else.

Sanders said quickly, "You'll never believe who was on the eastbound Super Chief that arrived in Los Angeles this morning. Clark Gable. I met him, too."

She smiled and said only, "That's nice."

"I can't believe this. *It Happened One Night*. It's my parents' favorite movie of all time."

"I hear a lot about how my movies are parents' favorites," she said coolly as she began to pivot around and away from Charlie Sanders. "I must get on with my script work."

He kept up with her. "May I ask you a question, Miss Colbert?"

She kept moving. "The answer is No."

"I'm so so sorry for even asking . . ."

She stopped and looked at Charlie Sanders. She was smiling. "I mean the answer to your question is No, young man of the Santa Fe. You want to know the same thing everyone else wants to know. The answer is: No. I did not sleep with Clark Gable while we were making *It Happened One Night* or on any other occasion—including our second movie together, *Boom*

Town, an awful thing about gushing oil in places like Texas. We were not a match either by attraction or inclination."

Sanders was happy that they were still in semidarkness. That meant this glorious woman of stage and screen and the world, Claudette Colbert, could not see the blush that not only infused his face but was deep down into the pores and cells of his being.

"No, ma'am, that was not my question," he hastened to say. "I would never ask such a personal question."

"Yes, you would. We of the movies are asked nothing but personal questions."

Now it really was good-bye, young man of the Santa Fe.

But Charlie Sanders had more questions. "Would you be interested in playing in a movie that took place entirely on the Super Chief?"

"Not in the least," answered Claudette Colbert. "I am not Gloria Swanson, I ride on the Super Chief but it is not an object of my passion."

"Do you know Susan Hayward?" Sanders persisted.

"Everybody in Hollywood knows everybody but nobody knows anybody," said Miss Colbert.

"Is she sick?"

She flicked the question off with a flip of a hand.

"What about John Wayne?" Sanders asked. "Is *he* sick?"

"There's not a disease in the world that would dare touch that man. Farewell, young man."

"Did you have a friend named Otto Wheeler?" Charlie

Sanders asked as Miss Colbert eased farther away. "That was my real question, ma'am."

"Friend? Otto Wheeler?" She was still walking, but slowly. "I didn't even have an enemy named Otto Wheeler. Who is Otto Wheeler? Was he an actor? A director?"

"He lived in Kansas—Bethel, Kansas."

The woman of the world laughed. "I am not Judy Garland either—I am really not Judy Garland." She said it with the clear message that she was most happy not to be Judy Garland. "I have never even been to Kansas."

Sanders looked out the large window on the left side of the lounge to the passing landscape. "You are now," he said. "This is Kansas."

"I am never in Kansas, young man," said Claudette Colbert in full vowel, not even tilting her head toward what might be outside the window.

Charlie Sanders remained as still as stone for at least a minute—maybe two or even more.

Even though Claudette Colbert had physically vanished from his presence, having disappeared back down the passageway, he remained paralyzed by her starry magic, her perfume, her vowels.

I just spent nine minutes in the dark with Claudette Colbert!

That's what he wanted to yell out a train window or telegraph to his mom, dad, little brother and every relative and friend in Garrison, Indiana, and everyone else everywhere.

Or sing it, dance it, leap it as if he were Gene Kelly or Donald O'Connor. Or a trapeze artist in a circus.

He knew this might very well end up being *the* experience of his lifetime.

We are gathered here today at the First Methodist Church of Garrison, Indiana, to honor the memory of Charlie Sanders of the Santa Fe who spent nine minutes on the Super in the dark with Claudette Colbert!

Sanders finally eased his way back to a chair at the very end of the observation car.

As he continued to yell silently to everyone everywhere.

She talked to me! Claudette Colbert called me "young man of the Santa Fe!" We had a conversation! I talked to her back! I called her "Miss Colbert"! She told me about a play she was going to be in! I asked her to be in a movie that happens on the Super!

He was still sitting straight up and wide awake at least half an hour later when he heard a noise and then saw the shadow of a person enter the dark lounge.

Charlie could tell only that it was a man. Claudette Colbert had not returned.

"May I help you, sir?" he said to the man, who was not clear enough to make out—or recognize. "It's me, Charlie Sanders of the Santa Fe."

After two beats of silence the voice said, "This is Rinehart of The End."

Sanders had no idea what Rinehart meant but he knew exactly what he was expected to do immediately.

"I was just leaving, Mr. Rinehart," he said. "I know you want your privacy here this time of night."

Rinehart had taken only two or three steps into the lounge and stopped.

Now, as he got closer, Sanders could see Darwin Rinehart clearly. "The conductor told me you had turned right back around at Los Angeles and headed east . . ."

"To die," Rinehart said, finishing the sentence in a soft whisper. "I came back on the Super Chief to die."

Charlie Sanders turned aside, preparing to walk by Rinehart and out of the lounge. In a flash, he remembered his bad-taste thought about Otto Wheeler of Bethel, Kansas, deciding to go The Chief Way.

"Now, Mr. Rinehart, let's not joke about things like that," Sanders said.

He and Rinehart were now facing each other in the dim light less than three feet apart.

"Not a joke, Charlie Sanders. Will you help me?"

"Mr. Rinehart, please," Sanders said, his mind racing now with thoughts about how weird it was that two Super passengers in two days had brought aboard with their luggage a desire for a suicide assist.

"Last night, same time, same place I tried but I couldn't do it," Rinehart said. "Without Gene I can't do anything—not even kill myself."

Rinehart said his post-midnight excursion twenty-four hours ago had been the only time he had left his compartment until now.

"Mr. Mathews seems like a really nice man," Sanders said. He could think of nothing else to say.

"I'm sure Gene would give you a job in pictures," Rinehart said. "Help me now and Gene will help you later."

Now there was another thing Rinehart said that didn't make sense. How was a dead man going to make sure his surviving friend honored any kind of commitment? But Sanders let it go with silence.

Rinehart told Sanders that last night about this same time he walked out of the lounge, past his own compartment to the vestibule between the observation car and the next sleeping car.

"We were speeding along through the California desert towns one after another. I thought I saw Needles, California, out there. Must have been Needles. Way too late for Barstow. What town comes next after Needles?"

"Kingman, Arizona. But the Super Chief doesn't stop there either—"

Rinehart held up a hand for silence. He knew where the Super Chief did not stop, thank you.

"I went to the side doorway on the right. There was the lever up there at the top, and another at the bottom that opens the door."

Rinehart closed his eyes. Sanders assumed he was trying to see himself standing in the open doorway.

"The wind from the train was blowing my hair and clothes as I counted to myself—one, two, three . . . jump!"

With his eyes reopened, Rinehart said, "I couldn't do it. Imagine it, yes. But do it, no. Not without Gene. Do you know about Willy Loman?"

"Yes, sir," Sanders said. "The salesman in the play—"

"He has more guts than I do, Sanders of the Santa Fe," Rinehart said.

Sanders of the Santa Fe knew he had a very serious problem on his hands—as a railroad employee, as well as a simple human being from Garrison, Indiana. Summoning up the authority he had gained from his phony detective experience, he said, "I will not permit you to take your own life on the Super Chief, Mr. Rinehart."

Rinehart put a hand on Sanders's shoulder and gave it a shove. "Leave me alone then."

Sanders walked out of the lounge, toward the narrow corridor of compartments.

"No train movies for you, kid!" Rinehart yelled after him.

Sanders stopped in that same between-cars vestibule where Rinehart said he had come last night. He pulled down the small folding stool that railroad crew use. There he would remain as a sentinel on behalf of the Santa Fe.

With his glass of scotch in hand, Rinehart made his way to a seat farther back in the quiet darkness.

In a few minutes Sanders was back.

"Sorry to bother you, sir," he said loudly toward Rinehart.

"But I wanted you to know that earlier tonight—right here, in fact—I happened to speak for a few minutes with Claudette Colbert. I asked her about the possibility of starring in a movie that happens on the Super Chief—"

"Go away, kid!" Rinehart yelled.

And before Sanders could actually go away, Rinehart added in a somewhat lower volume, "Relax, kid. I'm not going to do anything by myself. I can't."

That was enough for Charlie Sanders to keep walking past his sentinel post at the vestibule to a vacant roomette three cars up.

He was suddenly very tired. He needed to sleep—to rest.

Without Gene there had been no one to talk to. He had a couple of books and some magazines and a newspaper. What else was there to do besides stare out the window at pitch black, sand, lights and an occasional train station? But that staring, that being lost in the unknown of out there was part of the magic of the Super. Wasn't it?

Without Gene, he had decided he was not up to being seen or seeing. So both evenings he had Ralph bring him his martinis first and then his dinner—again, roast rib, baked potato, salad and red wine—to his compartment.

Now he sat there by himself in a private stupor, brooding over how he had failed to Jump!

He tried to consider again if Gene could be right about making a comeback. He had never been that far up, that famous or powerful to begin with, so the return wouldn't be that long a trip. Even if Gene was also right about *Elmer Gantry* and Burt Lancaster there was no way in hell he could get the rights, the backing or Burt. And forget trying to get Grant, Saint, Mason and Hitchcock or any combination like them to ever do anything for him. Comeback? No, forget it. Nobody in pictures comes back from the kind of humiliating bankruptcy he was going through.

They stole my house! My Brancusi!

Television? What would it take for him, inside his soul much less technically and professionally, to make a television series? Could he actually organize properties, scripts, writers, directors, actors, networks, flacks and whatever it took to make hundreds of formula half-hour programs about cute families, feuding couples, tough cops, honest lawyers, frantic doctors, dedicated teachers? Would that be better or worse than humiliating bankruptcy—or even death?

"Welcome, whoever you are."

It was a female voice. Rinehart adjusted his eyes to see a woman in sunglasses with a shawl over her head. She was smoking a cigarette.

"Thanks," he said. Company was not what he wanted—particularly right now.

"I'm Miss Scarlett," said the female voice. "Care to join me?"

He wanted to yell No! But there was something familiar in

her voice. And how in the world could he resist that name, Miss Scarlett?

Whatever else, this woman was probably Pure Hollywood, mused Rinehart as she sat down in one of the lounge chairs next to him.

"Don't look too closely," she said. "I'd prefer that you didn't recognize me."

There seemed little chance of that. The large scarf, which seemed to be dark blue—it was difficult to see for sure in the dark—and the sunglasses combined to make her face nearly invisible. All Rinehart could tell was that she was a mature woman of an indeterminate age with bright white skin who had coated herself in a strong-smelling perfume and filled herself with what smelled like gin.

She had set a glass of it in front of her. There was no ice in the glass, making it a perfect match with his own drink.

"What are you doing up and about at this time of night?" she asked.

That voice. It was definitely a lady of the movies—maybe a star of the movies. At least, she had a voice Rinehart had heard before.

"I always come in here about now," said Rinehart.

" 'Always come in here'? What does that mean?" she said. A few more sentences, thought Rinehart, and I'll know who she is.

"I'm a regular on the Super Chief, that's all," he said. "I like to come in here in the late dark and sip a scotch."

"For a while, I was a regular, not for long and no more," she said. "This is my first time in a long time."

Rinehart now knew exactly who this woman was. She was indeed a star—or had once been a star.

She said, "Do you want your drink refreshed? I've got more where this came from back in my compartment."

"No, thanks. I'm fine."

" 'No, thanks, I'm fine.' Well, that's easy for you to say. I'm not fine at all. I haven't had a role worth anything in five years. I'm quitting. I *have* quit. Everything I own is in the trunks I have with me on this train. I'm on my way to Europe. Sailing on the *Queen Mary* next week from New York. I'm going to live in Switzerland or someplace and I'm not going to even go to the movies, much less act in them. Do you blame me?"

"No, I do not. I know exactly how you feel and, as a matter of fact—"

"I could have gone away on an airplane. But I decided my last trip out ought to be on the train—the Super Chief. Old times' sake. Go slowly. Other reasons for the Super Chief, too. Personal reasons. I'm never coming back. The pictures got everything I had and they hate me. Everybody hates everybody else in Hollywood. Did you know that? Remember Harry Truman when he was president? He used to say that if you wanted a friend in Washington, get a dog. Well, let me tell you in Hollywood even the dogs will bite you in the back."

Rinehart smiled and then he laughed out loud, particularly at the idea that he hadn't known until they got to LA that

Harry S Truman himself had been on the westbound Super Chief.

She laughed, too, for her own reasons—probably at her telling of the Truman line. Then she made a move to stand.

"You're Grace Dodsworth," said Rinehart. "I'm Darwin Rinehart."

She sat back down. "Did we work on a picture together?"

"Yes. *The Tie That Binds* in 1941."

"Right, right. Set on Park Avenue. I was the killer—and I got away with it. I strangled Barton Greene with his own necktie."

"That's right. A red, white and blue one."

"But it was in black and white so nobody could see the colors. I was Rose. His character's name was Richard. The sonovabitch had stolen my daddy's inheritance, thrown it all away on the horses and the whores. I hated him for that. I hated him more than anybody I had ever hated before in my life . . ."

Her speech was not quite slurred but the words were becoming increasingly rounded—and loud. Rinehart couldn't tell if it was the gin or the anger that was the primary cause. Her ferocity recalled the conversation he'd had with Gene about actors playing out their make-believe roles. She sounds as if she really does hate the Barton Greene character. Wasn't she also married to the real Greene, the British actor? There was a time in Hollywood when it seemed everybody had been married to everybody for a while.

Rinehart said, "He came in falling down drunk, taking off

his suit coat and tie, you confronted him, he socked you in the jaw, you shoved him backward—"

"He fell back, but onto a couch—"

"A chair, actually."

"All right, a chair. He passed out. I grabbed the tie he had just taken off. I went around behind him, wrapped it around his neck and pulled it until he was dead. I strangled him and it was good riddance."

There was an element of stridency in her voice—as if she had just killed the guy a few minutes ago and was damned proud of it.

"I really did get away with it, too."

"You did indeed. You merely put the tie back around your dead husband's neck, tied it in a regular four-in-hand knot and the police never thought of it as the murder weapon. They suspected you might have killed him but nothing could ever be proved and it worked as a movie because it was a satire and he was such—"

"An awful bastard who deserved to die!"

"Exactly. You were terrific."

"My god . . . it's getting me all worked up. See, I can still do it. I can act. What's your name again?"

"Darwin Rinehart. I was the producer of that picture." He chose not to add the fact that her name was engraved on his silver *The Tie That Binds* flask with the rest of the cast. That flask was back in his compartment. Maybe he should get it and show it to her?

"Sure, right," said Grace Dodsworth. "Sorry. Yes, certainly you were. I remember you now."

"Nobody ever remembers producers." He laughed. It was not a friendly laugh.

"What happened to you since that picture?" she asked, but it was not a serious question. She didn't give a damn about him. She was just making noise. For him, the noise resonated deeply into his own thoughts about who he was and where he was right now.

He said, "I made seventeen pictures. We did have that one Oscar nomination for *The Tie That Binds* . . ."

"What time is it?" said Grace Dodsworth.

Rinehart said he couldn't see his watch in this darkness but it was probably well after one o'clock.

"Why don't you take off that scarf and those glasses?" he said. "I know who you are."

"Knowing is not seeing," she said. "If anybody sees me tonight on this train . . . well, it won't be you—or anyone from the movie business. It'll be somebody else."

Under normal circumstances, that would have sounded weird. But nothing was sounding that way to Rinehart right now.

Grace Dodsworth's was a well-known Hollywood story. She had been picked out of a nightclub chorus line when she was eighteen, given a screen test by MGM and established herself quickly as a sexy siren. She initially played mostly light roles with comedians such as Bob Hope and Jack Benny but then was given a chance to do some satirical stuff along the lines of *The Tie That Binds* and eventually a few serious parts. She was riding along on a star high when her personal life erupted into a series of storms. Her many affairs—some rumored with women as well as men—quick-short marriages, drinking and drug episodes took a toll.

The Super came to a gradual, gentle stop. Rinehart looked out the window. It was Bethel, Kansas, as he knew without even reading the sign in front of the station. Now he could see his wristwatch. It was just after one thirty.

Grace Dodsworth suddenly yanked off her scarf and sunglasses. She looked at her reflection in the window glass.

"How do I look?" she asked Rinehart—the world.

"Great," Rinehart replied. "Expecting someone?"

She didn't answer.

They remained seated, silent, staring out the window. The lights from the station and the platform at least had made the famous face of Grace Dodsworth fully visible to Rinehart. Her aging and drinking had left marks but her baby blue eyes and shiny porcelain complexion were as striking as ever. So was her hair, which was, with the help obviously of a coloring expert, still its famous reddish brown.

Finally, after five or so minutes, the Super eased away from Bethel, Kansas.

"I knew it was a long shot that he might be here tonight," she said as the Super picked up speed. "Life goes on."

Rinehart had no idea what she was talking about. He?

Who? Rinehart decided not to ask. He saw what appeared to be tears in her eyes. Whatever she meant, it seemed way too personal for him to ask about.

"Is there anything I can do for you, Miss Dodsworth?" he asked.

She shook her head. Then after a few seconds, she said, " 'Miss Scarlett.' Being a Hollywood man, you figured why I chose that name for this trip, am I right?"

She was indeed correct. He had definitely figured it out. But Rinehart decided to say nothing. This was her story.

"I'm the one Selznick really wanted for Scarlett O'Hara. But he couldn't cast me because I couldn't prove to the bluenoses I was really married to . . . oh never mind. You know all that."

Yes, Rinehart knew all that. Everyone knew all that.

He said, "As coincidence would have it, Clark Gable just came in on the westbound Super Chief from Chicago yesterday morning."

She shook her head again. "Couldn't be. I was with Clark—in the flesh, so to speak—in a suite at the Beverly Wilshire in L-A Land the night before, saying our farewells. Bad Breath and I used to be quite an item, and we were—one last time. He's still not much more of a lay than he ever was. Carole Lombard was right about his not being any kind of king in the sack. But who cares. It's Clark Gable. For me, like leaving town on the Super Chief, it was all for old times' sake."

Rinehart assumed that Grace Dodsworth was either so drunk the other night in Los Angeles or right now on this train that she was dreaming about having been with Clark Gable at the Beverly Wilshire.

"I would have been a great Scarlett with Clark," she continued. "A great Scarlett. I'd have won that Oscar instead of that Brit twit Vivien Leigh. All she was before was to be Larry Olivier's lay. She didn't deserve that part. I did. They'd still be talking about me if I'd gotten it. I'd have been great. It's still in me. Acting is still in me. It'll always be in me. But I'm not doing it anymore. Do you hear me?"

At that moment, Darwin Rinehart made a decision to do something about what was in *him*.

"I do hear you, I do believe you," he said. "You are one of the greats of the business and you will always be known and revered as such."

Rinehart stood up. "I remember that scene from *The Tie That Binds*. To me, that was one of the great movie scenes of all time—of *my* all time, at least. Do you remember the lines?"

Grace Dodsworth stood. "I remember every line I have ever had."

She glided into the aisle of the lounge car. Rinehart pushed his chair out, too, and placed her scarf around his neck as if it were his tie.

They faced each other.

" 'You still up?' " he asked, in his best impression of a 1930s drunk hustler named Richard.

" 'I know about the money—the women, the gambling,' " Grace Dodsworth said as Rose of Park Avenue.

" 'Shut up about it and everything else,' " Rinehart said, grabbing the scarf from around his neck and placing it on the table to the side, as if he were removing his tie.

" 'Don't tell me to shut up!' "

" 'You do what I say!' "

" 'Never again!' "

Rinehart threw his right fist toward Grace Dodsworth's chin, stopping in time to avoid any contact—just like in the movie.

But she reached forward with both hands and shoved him with great force. There was hate in her eyes.

He fell carefully back in the chair, closed his eyes and slumped his head down onto his chest. He had, in accordance with the script, passed out.

Grace Dodsworth snatched the scarf off the table, went back behind Rinehart and wrapped it tightly around his neck, leaving the two ends free.

Rinehart felt tension in the scarf.

She had grabbed the two ends and was pulling on them.

The pressure mounted.

He coughed.

He had trouble breathing.

His head filled with haze.

His last thought before losing consciousness was that maybe the Santa Fe kid was onto something with his idea about a movie that happens on the Super Chief. A remake combination of *Silver Streak* and *Grand Hotel*? Maybe there was a TV series here if nothing else. You could stretch one forty-hour Chicago-to-LA trip into eighty half-hours. But not with Claudette Colbert . . .

When the scene was over, Grace Dodsworth mouthed the word CUT!

Then she unwrapped the scarf, pulled it from around Rinehart's neck and tied it back over her head. She replaced her sunglasses, picked up her gin and walked back to her compartment.

She remained there for the rest of the night until, from the passageway outside, she heard shouts of alarm, calls for Detective Pryor to come immediately as the Super Chief completed its silvery streak to Chicago.

Jack Pryor immediately closed off the observation car, securing, as is, the body of Darwin Rinehart and any accompanying evidence there might be.

Then, through conductors and attendants, he ordered that everyone remain on the train upon arrival at Dearborn Station.

That happened ninety nonstop minutes later.

Pryor, after talking briefly to several crew members, had concluded that Rinehart's death must have occurred after the Super crossed the Mississippi River into Illinois—probably somewhere between Streator and Joliet. That meant the Rinehart death was the official business of the State of Illinois, a declaration Pryor made official with phone calls to local, state and railroad authorities once at the station.

Three hours later the coroner, forensic and other investigative personnel released Rinehart's body and an hour after that the passengers began to be told they were free to go.

The first allowed to leave were Claudette Colbert and Grace Dodsworth.

Epilogue

The Rinehart case remains officially open after more than fifty years.

There have been no developments since July 1956, when a Chicago coroner concluded after a three-month investigation that Darwin Rinehart was the victim of strangulation by "a means and person unknown."

Jack Pryor was not faulted by the Santa Fe for his handling of either the Rinehart or Wheeler deaths. He was also cleared of any wrongdoing in putting Dale L. Lawrence off the Super. Pryor went on to be deputy chief of the Santa Fe police, retired in 1972 and died ten years later of congestive heart failure.

Grace Dodsworth's last public appearance in the United States was in 1996 at the Kennedy Center Honors in Washington, DC. The strangling scene from *The Tie That Binds* was among the movie excerpts in her tribute film narrated by Elizabeth Taylor. Grace Dodsworth died of pneumonia two years later at age eighty-four in Lausanne, Switzerland.

Former Valerie County sheriff Hubert Ratzlaff resides in Otto Wheeler Village, a Randallite assisted-living facility in Bethel. In 1967 he judged the Wheeler killing as closed after a Chicago hit man named Ronald Allen ("Doak") Faulkner confirmed in open court that Wheeler was one of his fourteen for-hire victims. Faulkner was not forced to identify who hired him to kill Wheeler.

Faulkner's confessions were an add-on part of a deal to avoid the death penalty. He is serving life without parole at Stateville State Prison, next to the abandoned Joliet prison building now used as a rent-a-prison movie and TV set. "Doak" came from Faulkner's admiration for the famous football player Doak Walker.

Charlie Sanders never finished his "confession" to Jack Pryor or said a word about it to anyone else. He also did not pursue a job in Hollywood. After rising to be vice president of the railroad, he is retired and lives in Naples, Florida. There is no sign of any connection between his Super idea and the movie *North by Northwest*. Whatever happened, he felt—feels, still—he would have been owed no credit or anything else because he did what he did as an employee of the Santa Fe.

Claudette Colbert, a 1989 Kennedy Center Honors recipient, appeared in her last movie in 1961 but continued to act onstage and on television. She was ninety-two when she died in 1996 at her Barbardos home after a series of strokes.

Gene Mathews had no involvement in *North by Northwest* or *Elmer Gantry*. He left the movie business shortly after Darwin Rinehart's death. Mathews staged a memorial service at the Beverly Wilshire Hotel for his friend, providing a small ballroom with one hundred and fifty chairs, an elaborate buffet and a lot of red and white flowers. Only twenty-two people showed up.

Mathews died of leukemia in 1968, one of fifteen leukemia or cancer victims among the *Dark Days* Utah crew. Another was Tracy Thurber, the girl Rinehart discovered on a trolley. Ninety-one of the 220 who worked in Utah on *The Conqueror* also became cancer or leukemia victims. The forty-six who died included John Wayne, Susan Hayward, Agnes Moorehead, the Mexican actor Pedro Armendáriz and the director, Dick Powell. Moorehead, just before her death, said, "Everybody in that picture has gotten cancer and died." Her remark was ignored because most of the famous victims—Wayne and Hayward in particular—had been heavy smokers.

A. C. Browne did not publish anything about Harry Truman or the Super Chief trip, but he did write a brief personal memo on what Dale Lawrence had told him in Dodge City. In 1972 he scribbled on that paper, "S. Hayward dead! Must get on this. A.C.B." Albert Carlton Browne died from kidney disease a year later before acting on that instruction to himself. A bronze bust of Browne stands in a small park in downtown Strong, next to the *Pantagraph* newspaper office.

Nothing in the Truman presidential library mentions Browne, Dale Lawrence or the 1956 Super ride. But there is a note in Truman's own handwriting from a conversation he had with an Atomic Energy Commission official in 1971 about the Nevada tests. "Somebody's got to start thinking of compensation for these people!" he wrote. The former president died in December the following year. Compensation legislation was passed by Congress in 1990.

Truman and Browne had it right: Clark Gable was a phony. He was really Will Masters, founder and still the owner of The King's Motors, a Chrysler-Dodge-Jeep dealership in Janesville, Wisconsin. Masters was born with a striking resemblance to Gable, and he perfected the actor's speech and mannerisms as he grew older for social and, later, business reasons. Masters was egged on by a friend to put on a mustache, among other false things, and test his Gable role on the Super. Masters selected that specific 1956 Super westbound trip because he knew from the newspapers Gable was in California preparing to shoot another picture. Something about the Civil War with Yvonne De Carlo.

The blonde from Missouri who visited the Masters/Gable compartment went ahead with her I-had-sex-with-The-King boast. Her lawyer husband divorced her, and he was about to sue Gable until it was proved Gable was nowhere near the Super Chief that night. The woman lost her job with the Missouri lieutenant governor.

Ralph, the sleeping car porter, knew it was not the real Clark Gable. Ralph had been close to The King too many times before. But he had no reason to help Jack Pryor expose the man and, besides, he figured the phony was likely to give a larger tip than the real Gable. The imposter did give Ralph seventy-five dollars—a crisp fifty, a twenty and a five. Gable's usual amount was fifty. Ralph retired without ever being caught on a Private transaction or identified as the go-between for the Wheeler shooting. He lives now on a beachfront estate in the Virgin Islands.

The Super ended its thirty-five-year Santa Fe life on May 1, 1971, when the federal government, through Amtrak, took over. Santa Fe made Amtrak remove the Super Chief name when onboard service deteriorated, but Santa Fe partially relented in 1984 to permit what remains to this day as the Southwest Chief.

The full Super story has been preserved at the Museum of the Super Chief, the only institution of its kind in the world devoted to a single train. It is housed in the restored Santa Fe depot and Harvey House hotel/restaurant in Bethel, Kansas. A reconditioned Warbonnet diesel engine and seven cars of the Super Chief sit on a track next to the buildings.

In exchange for a tax-free contribution, the display train is being made available for two television projects—a cold cases story about the Rinehart death and a pilot for a fictional miniseries based on the Super deaths fifty years ago.

The Museum of the Super Chief is open to the public Tuesdays through Sundays, 10 a.m. to 5 p.m. April through October, 11 to 3 the rest of the year. Admission is $7.50—seniors $3.00, students free.

Acknowledgments

I needed a lot of help in walking my wavy lines between the real and the made-up.

I mined a variety of printed and video material—from newspaper clippings, Google entries and thick books to short documentaries and full-length feature movies. The details of *The Barbarians* saga came from Harry and Michael Medved's *The Hollywood Hall of Shame*. Gar Alperovitz's *The Decision to Use the Atomic Bomb* and David McCullough's *Truman* were important sources. So were *Super Chief. . . Train of the Stars* by Stan Repp, *Clark Gable* by Warren G. Harris, *Picture* by Lillian Ross, *Rising from the Rails* by Larry Tye and Frederic Wakeman's novel *The Hucksters*—plus the movie it spawned.

Bob LaPrelle, director of the Museum of the American Railroad in Dallas, was with me from the beginning. I visited a restored Super Chief dining car at the California State Railroad Museum in Sacramento. The Truman Library in Independence, Missouri, answered a call for assistance. So did Jan McCloud of the Newton, Kansas, police department, the folks at *The Emporia* (Kansas) *Gazette*, Sue Blechl of the Emporia Public Library and Chris Childers, a young man of Emporia research.

I am grateful to everyone involved and I hereby absolve them of any responsibility—or blame.

ABOUT THE AUTHOR

This is JIM LEHRER's twentieth novel. He is also the author of two memoirs and three plays and is the executive editor and anchor of *PBS NewsHour*. He lives in Washington, D.C., with his novelist wife, Kate. They have three daughters.

ABOUT THE TYPE

The text of this book was set in Janson, a misnamed typeface designed in about 1690 by Nicholas Kis, a Hungarian in Amsterdam. In 1919 the matrices became the property of the Stempel Foundry in Frankfurt. It is an old-style book face of excellent clarity and sharpness. Janson serifs are concave and splayed; the contrast between thick and thin strokes is marked.